SECOND TIME AROUND

SECOND TIME AROUND

The story of my heart transplant journey

Dr Rajeev Banhatti

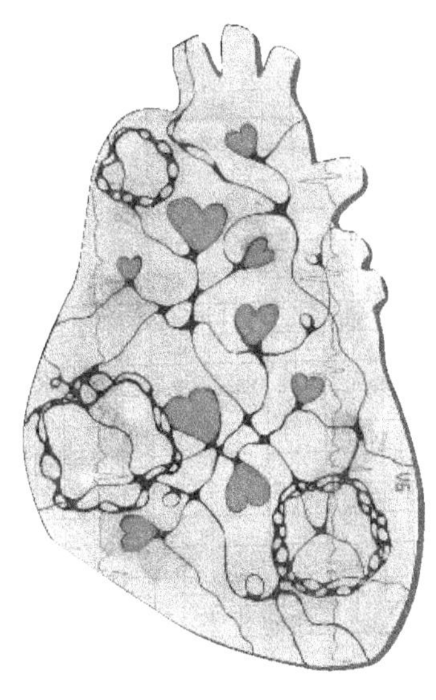

*We would like to dedicate this book to
donors and their families around the world*

Foreword

I was deeply touched and honoured when Seema Banhatti asked me to read the draft of this memoir and to write a foreword. This is a very personal story; that of Dr Rajeev Banhatti and his family, all of whom were profoundly affected by his illness. I had the good fortune to meet Rajeev and Seema about eleven years ago and to play a small part in the events that followed.

Once I started reading the manuscript, I found it difficult to put down. It is a very moving story and, despite my attempt at clinical detachment, it had a profound impact on me. In part, this was because I knew Rajeev and Seema. I also know that they fought a very difficult battle with great courage and fortitude. Despite all that he went through, Rajeev appeared surprisingly cheerful (although he probably did not feel that way). He was unfailingly polite and grateful for what little I and my colleagues could do for him. I will never forget our conversations about the books of P. G. Wodehouse or his attempts to get me interested in the Wallander novels (Scandi noir for those who haven't heard of them!).

Rajeev wanted his story to be of help to others navigating the difficult road of a chronic serious illness. I think it will serve this purpose. What struck me as a physician was how difficult it can be for a patient, even a doctor like Rajeev, to understand what is happening to him and to get timely help and support from the healthcare system when he needed it. Clinicians working in the healthcare setting would also benefit from reading this book. We need to remember that what may be 'routine' to us can be bewildering and frightening to a patient and to the family. We need to remember that time spent on explaining symptoms or the reason for a course of treatment is never a waste, and that we should be more than mere 'prescribers'.

Rajeev was very unfortunate to develop a serious health problem when relatively young. He was, however, fortunate in having Seema as his life's companion and his constant source of support through all the years of his fight for life. I wish his life story could have gone on for longer. I have no doubt that he fulfilled his stated aim to 'live life to the full before I leave'. We could all learn from his example.

Dr Jayan Parameshwar

September 2023

Acknowledgments

Our children give us strength, support and guide us when we feel like giving up. I am grateful to my children, Ruchi and Suhrud, my son-in-law Alex, my nephew Pradyumna and my sisters and brothers-in-law for encouraging me to compile Rajeev's writings and publish this book.

I would like to thank each and every person who had Rajeev and his wellbeing in their prayers and thoughts from the day of the diagnosis till the very last moments. That love was able to carry him through the toughest of the situations, and I am sure Rajeev would have agreed with me.

We are indebted with gratitude to the donor, his family and the hardworking and dedicated team of doctors, nurses and other medical staff of his specialist transplant hospital for making his incredible journey a reality, and also verifying the facts for this book.

The kindness and support from our close friends and colleagues from the UK and around the world has been invaluable throughout this journey.

Loving family members and close friends from all over the world were our constant source of strength and support at the other end of the phone, even when they were fighting their own battles.

Finally, I would like to mention two dear people, Joseph Pinto and Penny McCarthy, who believed we could write this story and made it happen.

Introduction

From my journal:

How to increase one's store/chance of happiness:

1. Satisfaction — common factor for poor or rich, healthy or unhealthy

2. Accepting one's own life course (so far, till the present moment)

3. Being responsible for what one chose, knowingly or (sometimes/often) unknowingly

4. Keep and care for your sense of humour. Do not undervalue it as pointless escape

In 2001, I was diagnosed with atrial fibrillation — a not uncommon condition, often relatively easily controlled. Nine years later, I developed a much more serious condition which would likely lead to death in two or three years without a heart transplant. This is the story of how I went from being a vigorous, healthy young man looking forward to a successful career in child psychiatry, to a weak, emaciated patient in need of major life-saving surgery — and beyond.

This book is for anyone facing similar challenges, their families and friends. In writing it, I hope to share my experience of a rare and difficult time, to provide a kind of roadmap that may help others to adjust. Of course, it isn't only the patient who travels this journey, and at several points in the story I have included Seema's account of particular events, to give some insight into how families who travel alongside their loved one are affected. This is her story too.

When I set out on my journey, I had no idea of the emotional toll that living with a heart condition would exact on me and those I love: the endless tests and consultations, hospital admissions, procedures and medications that are necessary to keep one alive; the repeated raising of hopes, only to have them dashed when symptoms return. Neither did I foresee the sometimes serious side-effects of treatment, nor the persistence needed to ensure that I received the most appropriate treatment. Each person's journey is unique and comes with its own obstacles and hardships. But with knowledge of the territory, even the darkest times may be less frightening. If this book helps just one person to find it less daunting, it will have been worthwhile.

I will forever be grateful to the National Health Service (NHS). The NHS is a vast, unwieldy organisation that can be difficult to navigate. My experience of it has not always been easy, but I am immensely grateful for the care I received – from the organisation and the many committed and compassionate individuals in it. Without their professionalism, my second chance at life would not have been possible. Medical professionals are human beings, with the same foibles and weaknesses as the rest of us, often working under nearly intolerable pressure. There are those who sadly lack the degree of compassion one might hope for. But I do not wish to criticise or blame any individual. For this reason, I have disguised the names of medical staff and hospitals mentioned in the book.

I'm grateful also to the family and friends who travelled this journey with me, prayed for me and supported me through the dark times. I'm glad that my parents had passed away before the serious phase of my illness began and were thus spared the anxiety and worry of those years. Despite the hardships, it has all been worthwhile.

It's impossible to understand why it took so long to begin writing this account; why it took over two years to write to my donor's next of kin. Maybe I needed that long to process it all.

This is my story . . .[1]

---

[1] Scattered through this account are quotations from other writers and from my own journal. Those of other writers are all credited in the text. The longer extracts from my journals will be obvious. Any unattributed shorter quotes are also from my journal.

Contents

Prologue

Chapter One   9/11 – Before and after

Chapter Two   The nightmare years

Chapter Three   Transplant

Chapter Four   Rejections, the highs and lows, and getting back to work

Chapter Five   Transcendent experience

Chapter Six   Retirement bites

Chapter Seven   Giving up or letting go?

Epilogue

Reminiscences of Rajeev from family and friends

Prologue

From my journal:

Expression of thoughts finds humanity's limits as well as hinting towards something beyond these limits when at its most effective.

An ordinary being like me can but express my thoughts with honesty and authenticity as far as I can manage it. Sometimes the process becomes magic, when the receiver/perceiver adds his own understanding to the emotions, which are the well-springs of all thoughts.

These are the timeless moments one witnesses on an experiential level that take one beyond the changing and limited existence that one has to forebear.

I was born in Dhule, India, in 1960. Both my parents were professors of English, and my father was a college principal. They were a progressive family for their time. My father's mother had seven sons and one daughter, and expected the boys to do the household chores the same as the girls, so they knew what it was like. While we children were still young, I have memories of living in two rooms of a hotel for a time – my father looking after the children in one room, while my mother studied for her Master's in the other.

My parents were aspirational for their children. I was told I could study engineering or medicine, and to apply for both.

Psychiatry appealed to my philosophical nature. So I secretly tore up the application for engineering and only sent off the medical school application! Fortunately, I got in.

I qualified as a psychiatrist, from B. J. Medical College, Pune, and worked for a few years in India. But my wish was to work with children – a field that was not well developed in India back then – and looked for opportunities to train abroad.

I had decided that sitting an entrance exam to prove your credentials just to be allowed into the UK (or a similar country) was below my dignity and above my 'work threshold' (not worth the work needed). But when I was invited to a psychiatry job in the UK as part of the Overseas Doctors Training Scheme, I had no excuses left. Everyone else I met expressed excitement about my opportunity to go abroad.

I arrived at Heathrow in January 1991 with two huge suitcases, almost no money and wearing an overcoat that my colleagues still remember with a big laugh. One cold, but fine, morning I caught a coach from Victoria to take up my post in York, and was received by a friendly, bustling lady that was my tutor's secretary. My wife, Seema, and daughter, Ruchi, followed two months later.

I had no idea then that, despite my intention to go back to India in a few years, circumstances would result in me settling in the UK for good. As they say, man proposes and God disposes.

Over the next few years, I attained Membership of the Royal College of Psychiatrists, achieving my goal of qualifying as a child psychiatrist. Later, I was honoured with a Fellowship of the Royal College of Psychiatrists. We now had two children, twelve-year-old Ruchi, and nine-year-old Suhrud. Soon we would return home . . .

Chapter One

9/11 - Before and after

'I worry about Mimmi, Daddy, Aaee and Baba[2]. They are all getting older and reaching the age when they will begin to need our help.'

Seema was right. We were taking a long, hard look at life so far, a conversation that had been continuing for several weeks. 'We have been here ten years now. Maybe it is time to go back to India and attend to family duties.'

Family ties in India are strong. As the youngest child, I was especially close to my parents, and I felt enormous gratitude to them for the loving support I had received growing up. It wasn't only duty – it was my wish to return and help support them in their declining years.

I sighed. 'You are right, Seema. I worry too. But I would like to get some consultancy experience before we return. To know how it feels. The locum post in Northampton is an excellent opportunity.'

It's Saturday afternoon. We crunch along the pebbles of Folkestone beach, while Ruchi and Suhrud entertain themselves, running after the waves, squealing with delight as the surging

---

[2] Mimmi was my mother-in-law. Aaee and Baba are the words for Mum and Dad in my native language, Marathi.

water chases them back up the beach. Life is good: I'm in a Senior Staff Grade job – my first experience in child psychiatry – with a hardworking, supportive team, some of whom will become lifelong friends. A little rented house by the sea makes a comfortable home for our family. The children are doing well in their primary school. But it's time for a change.

'I have an idea,' I begin tentatively. 'Perhaps you could start the process for us, take Ruchi and Suhrud back, get them settled in a new school. I can join you in a year or so when I have more experience.'

Seema pauses, looks out across the sea, then turns to me: 'It's a good plan, Rajeev. Yes. I will make arrangements'.

* * *

Our plan was working. I had rented a two-bedroom flat in Northampton, and Seema returned to India with the children. Ruchi was a bit rebellious – she objected to having to leave her friends and her grammar school, but both children were settling in their new school in Mumbai. We four had been so attached to each other that I spoke to them almost daily and faxed letters on a newly purchased infrared fax machine. This was not enough, so we spent a fortune on Seema and the children coming for short trips, or me going once or twice.

The work of a psychiatrist is rewarding, but hugely demanding of one's personal resources. Our patients often find the world a brutal and confusing place, and they need and deserve our full attention and empathy. Consultations are at least an hour, and each hour spent with a patient brings a minimum of another hour of ancillary tasks – referrals, requests for second opinions and more. Milan Kundera's beautiful words often came into my mind: *'for there is nothing heavier than compassion. Not even one's own pain weighs so heavy as the pain one feels with someone, for someone, a pain intensified by the imagination and prolonged by a hundred echoes.'*

But I felt valued and supported by my colleagues at Northampton Child Adolescent Mental Health Service (CAMHS). Always willing to discuss cases and share their accumulated wisdom with me, they ensured I gained as much experience as possible. It looked as if my labours would result in the hoped-for end as, after six months I was offered a substantive post of Consultant Child Psychiatrist.

* * *

At work

9/11 in 2001 – that day ended many lives. That day touched many others. When I think of it now, I realise in all honesty that it was also the day that started the serious epoch of my 'heart-warming' story.

On the fateful day of 11th September 2001, I was participating in a family therapy session. Oblivious to happenings elsewhere, we were in darkness behind a one-way screen, concentrating on observing the session in the next room.

We were about to finish when a colleague burst in and shouted: 'Do you know what's happening in the outside world? Come out now!'

We all watched the shocking and mesmerising, addictive drama of the twin towers being hit by the plane and the fire and the collapse.

The same evening, we attended a company presentation in a nearby hotel. Curiously, a young American guy I met in the bar was talking confidently about this being a CIA conspiracy, phony terrorist attack, etc.

Back in the flat, I saw the repeats of the 9/11 news and went to bed. The next day I was due to pick up a colleague to go to a conference. Standing on his doorstep, I suddenly began to experience palpitations and felt very unwell. My colleague and his wife saw my blue-tinged face and thought I was having a heart attack. They called an ambulance. At Casualty, a doctor diagnosed atrial fibrillation.

Fear and disbelief struck in equal measure. I was fit. When we went exploring or had to climb stairs, I was always first to reach my goal, Seema huffing and puffing behind me. My mind raced. I was in the UK, my family thousands of miles away in India. What would happen if I became seriously ill? What would become of Seema and the children?

I was admitted to hospital for investigations. Should I let

Seema know? I decided to save her an anxious wait and leave contacting her until the diagnosis was confirmed. But I had not counted on my devoted wife's intuition. Seema takes up the story:

9/11 - the whole world was in shock that day. The newspapers and news channels all over the world repeatedly showing the footage of the twin towers. It was so distressing to watch the terror attack in action.

I was in India with the children that year. We had planned to go back to India permanently, so we three had gone ahead and were staying with my parents. Rajeev was working in Northampton and was supposed to follow us by the end of the year.

He called us each evening. That evening he told me how shocked he was after watching the news. He sounded really troubled by the terror attack. We talked about the children and how well they were doing in school and promised to speak soon. The next day I did not hear from Rajeev. I thought he must be busy, maybe he would call later. The day after, I tried his home number a few times early in the morning. He didn't pick up. Usually, he left for work at 8.45 am. I wondered why he wasn't picking up. My gut was telling me something was not right.

I decided to call his work number. I had met the secretaries in the office before, and they were friendly and helpful. One of them picked up the phone. I said, 'Hi Naina! How are you?' and we spoke about the attack and how shocking it was. Then I asked her, 'How is Rajeev?' For a moment, I couldn't believe her reply. She said, 'Rajeev is recovering well. He has had an EKG and an angiography and they will get the results soon. I didn't let her know how shocked I was. Just calmly asked her if it was possible to call and talk to him in the wards, and got the number from her.

Soon I found out everything that had happened. By the time I called that morning, he had been through all the tests. The results confirmed that he had arrhythmia. My dear husband, who always cared for me more than himself, had tried to save me from worrying from across the seven seas. I was so dumbfounded and worried, and could not even be angry. He was so far away and all alone. I told him never to keep such things from me in the future. We were together in everything, for better or for worse.

This episode made me understand the meaning of a southern African word, 'Ubuntu'. Literally, it means 'humanness'. To have Ubuntu is to be a person who is living a genuinely human way of life, pricing human relationships above everything. My husband's pure and genuine heart was so troubled by the inhuman action of 9/11.

* * *

From that time on, I was never to have lasting freedom from serious health problems; the next few years became a story of living with increasing uncertainty of a regular or irregular heart rhythm. The electrical impulses in my heart had become disrupted. Instead of beginning in the sinoatrial node, they were beginning somewhere else in the atria, making the heart quiver or twitch – fibrillation. This led to the palpitations and fluttering sensation I had experienced that evening. If fibrillation continues: *'The disorganised signal spreads to the ventricles, causing them to contract irregularly and sometimes quicker than normal. The contraction of the atria and ventricles is no longer coordinated and the ventricles may not be able to pump enough blood to the body'.*[3]

The cardiologist did not seem particularly concerned, and discharged me from hospital after a couple of days with lifestyle advice: 'This is a relatively common condition, not life-threatening in itself. For many people, it comes and goes and they learn to live with it. We only treat it if it persists for more

---

[3] www.hopkinsmedicine.org

than forty-eight hours. Reduce stress and look after yourself. Stay away from red wine. We'll have you in for a check-up every six months.'

But as a doctor, I knew that atrial fibrillation can lead to more serious conditions – stroke and heart failure. And a history of cardiac problems in my family put me at greater risk than average.

For a lover of white wine, the ban on the red variety was no hardship. In normal times, not separated from Seema by thousands of miles, I benefited from her excellent cooking; healthy food was never in short supply. We worked well together, our home life happy and relaxed. My secretary at CAMHS was efficient and kindly. But my patients deserved everything I had to give. Stress was inevitable, and knowing I had a heart condition only added to it.

* * *

For a while, the episodes of fibrillation were mercifully brief. However, uncertainty concerning my health was to become a constant companion . . .

It's early morning, a few months after my diagnosis. I wake in the bedroom of my Northampton flat. In the half aware-ness between sleep and waking, something feels wrong. Have I been dreaming? No. The palpitations have returned. With a jolt, I'm suddenly fully awake. I sit up in bed. Yes, there's no doubt. No need to panic, Rajeev, I tell myself, this has happened before; it will pass.

I perform the morning routines of washing and dressing, eat my porridge, and go down to my car, parked in the street outside my flat. Descending the stairs to the ground floor, my breath is laboured.

I see my patients, confer with colleagues, smile, complete the paperwork, trying to ignore the restlessness that comes with the palpitations and the strange, uneven heartbeat. Trying to keep my breath steady, to fend off the fear. I return to the flat, weary and fatigued. The next day it's the same, and the next. Just getting myself to work is exhausting. Concentrating on what I must do takes all my willpower. No doubt now. My heart is in fibrillation again. I contact my doctor.

It is decided that I should undergo electrical cardioversion, a procedure where controlled electric shocks are used to restore the normal pattern of heartbeat. The procedure can be performed at my local hospital. Almost like magic, the palpitations cease and my breathing is steady. I feel much more relaxed and breathe a sigh of relief. But I'm beginning to doubt the wisdom of our planned return to India.

* * *

A smiling Seema brings in the meal of pithala-bhaat from the little kitchen in the flat in Northampton. Heaven! What delicious aromas! I breathe in, savouring the scents of turmeric, green chilli and coriander. The canteen at work is tolerable, but, deprived of Seema's cooking, I have been in a kind of gourmet depression. I delight in the smells and flavours of my native land.

The children are at last sleeping peacefully in the spare bedroom. They have been excitable all day, but now we are alone.

For a while, we eat in companionable silence. Then Seema brings up the subject we've both been avoiding. 'Something is troubling you, Rajeev. What is it?'

When I married Seema fifteen years earlier, I had said: 'Expectations are not good. Expectations bring unhappiness'. Now I had to live up to my exhortation. I had planned my life and career, expecting to return to India to set up in private practice. But it seemed that fate, or God, had decreed otherwise.

I begin the little speech I've been preparing for this moment, 'Seema, I have been thinking about our future – our future as a family and my professional future.'

She stops eating and looks at me, a small smile on her face. I soldier on. 'I am forty. Most of my peers in India are established in their practices with their support circles. Coming in from the outside at this late stage might prove difficult. I must decide whether to go back and attempt to break in, or stay here where I already have a Consultant job. If we–'

'Rajeev, stop. I understand. I have observed your B J Medical School classmates while I have been in India. How they are settled in their practices with their networks. I too have been wondering if it would work for you to return now.'

Relief floods through me. How blessed I am to have such a wise wife! Neither of us mentions my health. It's not a major factor, but starting again at home would undeniably increase my stress levels. This is not what we intended. But in that moment, we both know that staying here, where I already have a job, is the right decision.

It is not made without a sense of guilt: I will not be alongside my parents as they age, not be quite the model son I aspired to be.

Life was certainly not turning out as expected.

* * *

Despite that, we had much to be grateful for. Seema and the children returned permanently, and we bought a house on the edge of Northampton – somewhere we could make into a home after the years of moving around, living in rented accommodation. I had a good relationship with the Northampton team, and I hit on an idea for instituting regular social occasions outside of work . . .

I open the door to another of my colleagues and his wife. 'Welcome! Please, come in and let me offer you a glass of wine – it's one of my specials!'

We enter the living room, crowded with colleagues and their wives. There is a pleasant buzz of animated conversation. I spot Seema moving unobtrusively among our guests, offering drinks and putting them at their ease. I catch her eye and she comes over. 'Seema, please meet my esteemed colleague, Bill Harmby.'

Her smile is warm. 'It's wonderful to meet you – Rajeev talks about you so much.'

'Nothing bad, I hope!' he replies.

'Seema is an excellent cook; she has prepared a traditional Indian celebration meal for us. It will be a treat.'

Over the meal, I open one of the special bottles of Sauvignon Blanc I've set aside for the occasion. When they all have a little in their glass, I begin: 'Now everyone, take your time. Swirl the wine in your glass, bring the glass to your nose and breathe in. Savour the aroma ... Now, take a sip – just a sip, mind you, and swirl it round in your mouth. What do you taste? ...'

Later, one of my colleagues stands. 'I'm sure you'll all agree this has been a wonderful evening: I would like to propose a toast – to Rajeev and Seema.'

'To Rajeev and Seema', they chorus. Warmth floods through me. The evening has been a success.

When the guests have departed and we're sharing a last glass of wine together, we talk it over. 'You have done something wonderful for them, Rajeev, bringing them together in this way.'

Life had not turned out how we expected but, as I prepared for bed that evening, I reflected that there are many paths to happiness.

It seemed that I was settled for the long term. But change often comes unbidden. By 2006, workplace politics led to a situation that made me uneasy about my position at Northampton CAMHS; a second cardioversion the same year failed to resolve my atrial fibrillation . . .

A typical anonymous hospital treatment room. Bland, neutral-coloured walls. The usual antiseptic smells that get into the back of my throat. The paraphernalia of test equipment.

Sitting on the examination couch in a green hospital gown, I listen, stunned, to the woman cardiologist, a tall Amazon of a Scottish woman, saying no point in repeated electro-cardioversions, her brusque manner disregarding of the shock of this pronouncement. It's 2006 and once again I'm on the roller coaster of uncertainty.

Having delivered this bombshell, she deigns to inform me that there is another alternative – radiofrequency ablation – which might work in the longer term. But it can't be done in Northampton. I will have to go to Oxford. More waiting for appointments, more waiting for tests and their results before the procedure can go ahead.

A catheter will be inserted into a blood vessel in my groin and threaded up to my heart, giving access to its interior. The area where the problem is located will be burned, creating scar tissue which will – hopefully – prevent the heart from conducting the abnormal electrical signals that cause the fibrillation. It sounds like torture, but the Oxford cardiologist is reassuring: radiofrequency ablation has an excellent record of preventing repeated episodes of atrial fibrillation.

* * *

Several weeks after the procedure, I am feeling myself again and the prospect of a long-term resolution of my problems lifts my spirits. And there is exciting news. On hearing of my situation at CAMHS in Northampton, I'd been head-hunted by the senior consultant at Kettering CAMHS. Imagine my delight, handing an envelope to my boss, who is no doubt thinking, 'Here's Rajeev with another request for resources', only to find it is my resignation!

My atrial fibrillation is under control and I am once again in a post where I feel valued. For the first time in a while, my future looks more certain.

There is still a lingering guilt about not being in India to help look after our parents. But my spiritual seeking has led me to a resource that will enable me to draw on a deep well of inner strength and resilience.

***

I had occasionally experienced brief moments of the sense of oneness known in Indian philosophy as samadhi since I was quite young, and had long wished to learn meditation and pursue these experiences more deeply. In 2006, I attended a ten day Vipassana meditation retreat. Vipassana is an intensive course in Buddhist meditation, intended to kick-start a lifetime's practice . . .

'Are you alright Rajeev?'

'Yes, I'm fine.'

'You've been so quiet since you returned.'

It's two days since I arrived home from the Vipassana course. I bask in the glow of the sun streaming through the conservatory windows, and savour the aroma of the morning cup of tea, the warmth of my love for my wife. Everything feels very intense. Gratitude floods my soul, and I discover there is a huge smile on my face: 'I want you to do the course too, as soon as you are able.

'It has changed me somehow. I can't describe it . . . all the worries that used go around in my mind . . . things I couldn't do anything about . . . now I can accept it's just how it is. And there is so much to be grateful for. How sad not to enjoy the pleasures of life because I'm worrying about things I can't change!'

It was true. Nothing in my life had changed in the ten days I'd been away. But I had returned with a new capacity to accept what I couldn't change – my own health problems, the failing health of our parents – and a resolve to expend my energies only on those things I could change. In doing so, I would reduce my own suffering and be of more use to those around me.

The experience had brought a degree of peace, despite everything that was happening. I continued to meditate and read widely about Buddhist philosophy. These discoveries would be my sustenance and support through the trials that were to come.

* * *

For now, the worst was behind us. Seema and the children enjoyed life in Northampton. My work at Kettering both challenged and rewarded. A senior colleague had set up an international charity to deliver workshops, and I joined him in this endeavour, offering lectures and workshops in India – a way of giving back, especially as I no longer intended to return permanently. Our children were growing up into thoughtful and responsible young adults. We had financial security, and I could indulge my passions for technology, music, and the novels of P G Wodehouse.

I had come to accept my fate in continuing to live thousands of miles away from my family, but when Aaee passed away in August 2008, my grief was intense. The pain of knowing that you will never again hold the hand of the one who brought you into the world and nurtured you to adulthood comes to us all, but is no less painful for being universal. The guilt of feeling I hadn't been the good and dutiful son I aspired to be only intensified my pain. My father had previously suffered a stroke and, although still mobile, needed considerable support with his physical needs. Now, bereft of his life companion as well, he very much wanted to come and live with us. Unfortunately UK law did not allow this. So instead, from 2008 until his death in 2011, for six months of every year, Baba came to stay with us on a tourist visa, returning to India and the hospitality of other family members for the other six months, for which I am grateful. It was undoubtedly an added chore, getting him up each morning, washing and dressing him before I went to work and getting him to bed each evening after a demanding day of work with psychiatric patients, but it was what I wanted - to care for him and make the most of the time together in his declining years.

Then came the return of symptoms of atrial fibrillation. Palpitations, breathlessness and fatigue, making even the simplest of everyday activities a trial.

There is a film – you may know it – 'Groundhog Day', where, each morning, the protagonist wakes to the exact same sequence of events he experienced the day before. And the day before, and the day before, stuck in an endless cycle of reliving the same events over and over.

Sitting in the cardiologist's room that autumn, I seemed to be having my own personal Groundhog Day, fated to re-live the same scenario endlessly through eternity. The same symptoms, the same location, the same actors, the same dialogue: 'We'll have you in for another ablation procedure. It's a very effective treatment …'

Had I not heard this before? Two cardioversions, and now a second radiofrequency ablation required two years after the first, despite having been told it was a long-term solution. I did not know that even this would not be the end of the story where problems with my heart were concerned.

Bringing myself back to the room, I manage to recover my equanimity, and smile at the consultant, 'Thank you so much, I appreciate everything you are doing for me.'

For the next couple of years, all seemed well. Then in 2010, it was Seema's turn to lose a parent, our beloved Mimmi. Again, our grief was accompanied by the pain of not having been alongside her during her declining years. Later in the year, the breathlessness and fatigue of atrial fibrillation re-turned, and I underwent what will always be to me, the 'bad ablation' . . .

As I walk away from the treatment room, I know all is not well. Breathlessness, if anything worse than before. Don't judge too soon, Rajeev. Perhaps it will take a little time to settle down.

I refrain from expressing my fears to Seema. No point in worrying her unnecessarily. But in the days that follow, it is clear that, this time, the ablation procedure has not worked. My breathlessness is worsening. I become unable to walk more than a few hundred yards without having to stop and rest. Getting to work, even moving around my own home, turn into a constant struggle. And in the weeks and months until my next appointment, the question of what my future holds is an ever-present companion to the soundtrack of my life.

In June 2011 we lose Baba. I feel my heart will break. It is natural to grieve at such a time, natural to wonder, why? Questions arise in my mind: Why is God tormenting me like this? When will this torture of my body and soul end?

There is a seemingly interminable wait for the gears of the NHS machine to turn, allowing me to progress to the next stage of the journey and an answer to the question of what now? More uncertainty, more appointments and investigations. More months of struggling to maintain the semblance of normal life. Until one dark day in October 2011, a year after the 'bad ablation', I am given my diagnosis. Restrictive cardiomyopathy.

Was it my fate to endure blow after blow for eternity? Seema, always my rock, took the news with her usual determined positivity.

A page from her diary:

A couple of months prior to my forty-seventh birthday in 2011, I realised I was going to reach fifty soon, and wanted to do something different, something adventurous. How about focusing on my much neglected fitness for a few months and planning a trekking trip into the Himalayas? That idea was very appealing. I felt happy and excited about my decision. Wonderful! I had a new goal! Something new to look forward to.

We were at the stage of life where I had the satisfaction of fulfilling my duties towards my family and my in-laws. Looking after them till they embarked on the final journey of their lives, guiding our children and seeing them succeed in their chosen career path.

Such a feeling of relief and fulfilment. I took a few deep breaths and thought, now is the time to start living life for ourselves. Plan things to do for Rajeev and myself, which we never had time for. However, life had other plans.

Rajeev had suffered from a heart condition - 'atrial fibrillation' for a few years and had undergone three procedures of radio frequency ablation over the last five years. It was managed with other medications, too. Since his last ablation in 2010, he had been experiencing a little more shortness of breath, tiredness. The cardiologist appointment for review was on 11th October 2011. I still remember that evening when Rajeev came home and we discussed the outcome of the appointment and the diagnosis.

He sat me down and said, 'I have been diagnosed with a rare heart condition called "restrictive cardiomyopathy". The walls of my heart are losing elasticity and becoming rigid. That is what is causing the increased shortness of breath and fatigue as the heart's pumping action is affected.'

I sat still. My heart was pounding. I was all ears. So nervous about what was coming next. New medications, perhaps another procedure?

He took a pause and said, 'There is no cure. The consultant said the only option is a heart transplant.'

We looked at each other and there was stunned silence for a few minutes. A feeling of extreme sadness swept over me. I felt numb and helpless with fear for the future.

What? How? Why him? We had just dealt with the blow of his dad's demise three months ago and this was our time to live life for ourselves. I thought life was being so unfair, but at the same time realised we still had each other.

Life always throws a curved ball when you are least expecting it. Now it was our turn to decide how to tackle it. Get out or face it. Go on a new adventure!

Second Time Around

18

Chapter Two

The nightmare years

Is life meaningless? Is suicide meaningless? I think living is the be all and end all for all. Nothing is meaningless, as things exist. Full stop.

Word is a mere invention of human beings. Human beings have a tendency to spend a long time thinking or talking about non-issues.

I think living, 'staying alive' is the meaning across the board, from humans, animals to plants — all the living things that exist. It has the quality of a very strong obsession or a primal, instinctive reflex. Why? Does anyone know? Apart from saying that it's the law of nature, or dharma, or God's will? And how? That is also difficult, as we know some of the physical mechanisms of survival and passing on of the genes, but do not know where we get the intention to want to cling to life.

Restrictive cardiomyopathy: a condition where: *'the walls of the main heart chambers become stiff and rigid and cannot relax properly after contracting. This means the heart cannot fill up properly with blood. It results in reduced blood flow, and can lead to symptoms of heart failure, such as breathlessness, tiredness and ankle swelling, as well as heart rhythm problems'*.[4] It can be inherited.

---

[4] www.nhs.uk/conditions/heart-failure

It shouldn't have been a surprise, given my family history. But I was in shock. My already palpitating heart pounded. Despite my suspicions, the cardiologist at my local hospital had to explain twice before his words registered.

'This is a lot to take in, Rajeev.' He continued, his voice gentle: 'Many people who have a restrictive cardiomyopathy will have mild heart failure which can be well controlled with medication, but your condition is too advanced. There will be plenty of time for your questions, but I'm afraid the only option now is to refer you for a transplant. Without a new heart, you have only two or three years left. With a transplant, there's a chance you might get ten.'

A dark cloud descended; I had been handed a death sentence. But wait … I replay his words in my mind: *'With a transplant, there is a chance you might get ten years.'* There is also hope.

At the very moment I needed them, other words I had once read came to me: *'If you can solve the problem, then what is the need of worrying? If you cannot solve it, then what is the use of worrying?'*[5] There was something that could be done. Banishing the dark cloud, I focused on what the doctor was saying.

There were two transplant waiting lists – the routine list and the urgent list. As we came to know later on, to qualify for the urgent list in the UK, the patient has to need continuous in-patient treatment (usually with inotropes or a mechanical pump). At this time I did not fulfil those conditions, so I would be placed on the routine list.

I would come to understand the irony of that assessment: starved of nourishment, my other organs would become weaker and weaker. By the time I became eligible for the urgent list, it was realised I might no longer be fit for major surgery.

But all that was in the future. I was just fifty-two. My children, nineteen and twenty-two, were still in university. So young.

---

[5] Shantideva's Bodhicaryavatara, or 'Guide to the Bodhisattva's Way of Life'

They needed me. Seema needed me. There was no decision to make; I was referred to a transplant centre.

Another six months of processing by the NHS. Was I fated to live my life in fear and uncertainty? More than ever, I needed to discipline my mind and follow the Buddha's exhortation: '*not to mourn for the past, worry about the future, or anticipate troubles, but to live in the present moment wisely and earnestly.*' Once again, I must gather my resources and accept what was happening. Facing it was the only option.

As I was to discover, it would be a long road and I would be much sicker before I received my new heart.

* * *

February 2012 – I had accepted an invitation to lecture at the Indian Psychiatric Society. The journey would not be easy in my condition: breathless, legs swollen with excess fluid as my kidneys struggled to cope with the insufficient blood supply. But I was proud to be asked to share my knowledge and experience with colleagues at home. The trip also gave us the opportunity to visit Ruchi, who was completing a work placement for her training as an Ayurveda practitioner (traditional Indian medicine), and consult with an Indian cardiologist friend.

How wonderful to be back in India! To experience again the noise, colour and excitement of my native country and the trip proved to be worth all the discomfort.

The day of my appointment with the cardiologist, unknown to me, he was observing me from his window as I walked to his office with Seema. Noting my grossly swollen legs, his response was immediate: why hasn't this man been given more diuretics? On our arrival he told me: 'They seem to be treating you very conservatively. We need to increase your diuretics. They will take the water away and the load off the heart.' My brother-in-law, who is an anaesthetist administered the diuretics intravenously at home, relieving me of five litres – five kilos – of water! I was still seriously ill, but the procedure improved my mobility and made the rest of the trip far more comfortable.

My lecture was well received; I felt honoured to contribute to knowledge of child psychiatry in India in this way. We went on to visit Ruchi, calling in at our village of origin, called, just like us, Banhatti! All possible because of the Indian cardiologist's intervention.

While visiting Ruchi, I had another consultation, this time with one of her Ayurveda tutors. We had asked the transplant centre if they had any objection to my taking alternative treatment, along with their prescriptions. The young cardiac surgeon we met at that time said his family believed in Ayurvedic medicine and if we felt it would help, it was fine to go ahead. So I returned to the UK with Ayurvedic medicines and lifestyle and dietary advice to complement the conventional drugs I was already receiving.

I arrived home in a more positive mindset, and suggested to Seema that we make the most of it, so we went to Morocco for four days too! She encouraged me to make a bucket list. As I reviewed my life to that point, I was filled with gratitude: 'I have had so many wonderful experiences, I can't think of anything to go on my bucket list because what other people live in a hundred years, I will live in fifteen years. I'm happy with my life. I just want to live every day I have.'

* * *

On our return, I was seen at the transplant hospital and, as expected, put on the routine list.

A specialist nurse explained the process: 'There are two teams of co-ordinators, which are completely separate, the donor team and the recipient team. When a heart becomes available, the donor team goes immediately to collect it, and the recipient team brings the patient in and prepares them. It could happen at any time, so you must always be ready. You'll get a call and a car will come to pick you up. They will wait for you and bring you in so the operation can take place as soon as possible.'

It was a beautiful picture he painted for us. Seema and I looked at each other nervously. My lips twitched with a tentative smile. Tears pricked my eyes and my heart pounded, this time with excitement. At last – an end to the years of ill health and uncertainty.

Sadly, this glorified picture of my heart transplant never became a reality.

* * *

I needed to stay as healthy as possible. The Ayurvedic treatment and advice supported me physically and emotionally. Diet very simple – no spices, the only flavourings green chillies, ginger and cumin. No wine at all! No cheese, no chocolate. I bought a treadmill so I could keep exercising at home. In photos from that period, I look thin, but healthy, and the possibility that a heart might become available at any time kept me in a positive mindset.

* * *

June 2012, the weekend of the Queen's Diamond Jubilee. On Saturday afternoon, as I prepare to leave for our planned celebration with friends, I'm struck by nausea and an overwhelming pain in my head. I grab the bedside cabinet in an attempt to counteract the frightening sensation that I'm falling over. Into the roiling mass of pain and nausea, the sound of a million buzzing hornets explodes inside my head. Overwhelmed, I drop onto the bed, where Seema finds me five minutes later.

The next few hours are a haze of pain, tinnitus, nausea and vertigo. At A&E, the bank holiday skeleton staff are kind enough, but the four-hour wait to be seen by a doctor is four hours of torture and fear. What is happening to me? Is this another serious illness?

* * *

As I was to discover, the inner ear infection was a side effect of the high levels of drugs needed to keep my blood-starved organs functioning. It resulted in the loss of ninety-five per cent of the hearing in my right ear and forty per cent in the left. (A few years along the line we learned that it had also affected my proprioception - the brain's ability to know where our body is in space - resulting in mobility difficulties.) But I was determined not to let these setbacks diminish my enjoyment of the many pleasures life still offered – the company of those I loved, reading, listening to music, indulging my passion for technology. But the effort to maintain normality in the face of debilitating symptoms was taking its toll.

I often felt during this time that, however normal I looked from the outside, no-one could fully understand what it was like for me. Some of us are blessed with natural empathy, but in reality we each tread our own path, and long-term illness is a lonely one.

Breathless and fatigued as I was, driving to work each day became more and more exhausting. Day by day it was increasingly difficult to get up and force myself out of the door. Seema and my wonderful secretary did their best to look after me and relieve me of every possible burden. A disabled badge meant I could park nearby at the hospital. But my muscles were now so shrunken from lack of blood there was no longer any question of exercise. And I was tired. Tired of trying to hold on, tired of trying to stay strong.

In late 2012, I decided to give in gracefully and retire on grounds of serious ill health. I asked Seema to stop working too, so we could make the most of the time together. I finished my last day at work in March 2013, eighteen months after being told I had only two or three years left without a new heart. Unless a donor heart was found, I was facing the growing certainty of physical death. Now I was experiencing professional death too.

* * *

We sit at the kitchen table. Food, once a great pleasure of life, has become one more method of torturing my failing body.

'What would you like for lunch, Rajeev?'

'I'm not hungry.'

'You need to keep your strength up.'

It's easy to feel that Seema just can't understand what it's like for me. But in a moment of empathy I realise the depth of the pain she too suffers, and I'm overcome with gratitude for her steadfast loyalty and patient efforts to make sure I stay as healthy as possible for the day the call comes.

I glance up at her, seeing the love and concern in her gentle eyes.

'I'll try some bread.'

She watches, mute, as I laboriously chew, then attempt to swallow, a tiny morsel which, for some reason, won't go down. Hoping that this time it won't regurgitate via my nose.

I reach out and touch her hand. She smiles and we nod in silent empathy.

* * *

The last year before I received my new heart was a living hell. So many pleasures denied me. Eating to fuel my body was now just an arduous necessity. Going to restaurants, once such a pleasure, became an embarrassing display of my vulnerability due to sudden nosebleeds and swallowing difficulties. At the time we didn't know that this latter was due to the insufficient blood supply to the muscles involved in swallowing. And there was another reason restaurant outings became a kind of ritual humiliation; as my mobility became poorer, the location of the toilet was an essential piece of information . . .

A restaurant in Northampton. We sit at a corner table with friends. It's early. As yet only a few tables are occupied. The only sound, apart from our quiet conversation, is of a waitress laying out cutlery. Low level antique-effect lamps create a soothing ambience. It's good to be out of the house.

A cheerful-looking waitress comes over to offer us menus. As she's about to go, I remember to ask: 'Excuse me, is there a toilet on this floor?'

She grins, then says at a volume loud enough for everyone in the restaurant to hear: 'Sorry, no. But I can bring you a pot to pee in if you like!' and bounces off to the kitchen, laughing loudly at her own joke.

It's like a punch in the stomach. I don't know where to look – not at our friends, not at the other customers. Not at Seema, who will be as embarrassed as I am. I decide that being upset will not improve the evening for any of us. The best way to maintain my dignity is not to react to what feels like a deliberate insult, but to remain calm: 'Seema, what would you like to eat?'

* * *

The transplant centre checked in every few months, but as time went by, I began to feel I was being left to wither away and die. Living with growing uncertainty was a strain on us both, and the promised psychiatric support never materialised. Fortunately, I had my psychiatry training to fall back on – a case of *'physician heal thyself'*. And Buddhist philosophy always proved an alternative perspective. In dark moments, I would remember to pause and take a step back, accept things as they were. I would find solace in re-reading a P G Wodehouse novel, watching some Scandi noir, indulging my passion for cricket, or listening to some of my favourite blues music. I had so much to be grateful for – my lovely home with Seema, her unstinting love and loyalty; my wonderful children who showed such strength and were such a support to their mother; good friends who prayed for us and helped keep up our spirits during those years.

Even in the darkest of times, there are always moments of happiness; in 2012 Ruchi had graduated with her degree in Ayurveda and in May 2013, her boyfriend, Alex, proposed to her while they were on holiday in Japan and we threw a small party for close friends and family. Later that summer we proudly watched as Suhrud received his degree in product design engineering at Swansea University. It gave me a warm glow to know that my children were making progress in the world, that Ruchi and Alex were committed to each other and that my darling daughter was taken care of.

* * *

December 2013 – two years since going on the transplant list. Since being told that, without a new heart, I only had two or three years left.

Despite, or maybe because of, my multitudinous physical problems, I had an intense desire to experience India again before the operation. We planned our visit, along with Ruchi, Alex and Suhrud, to coincide with my nephew's wedding in the December.

It was a trip of contrasts – difficult family dynamics and a lack of understanding of my frailty caused some uncomfortable moments. There were blessings too – seeing Daddy – Seema's father, and my dearest friend Sharad from medical school days. He too was seriously ill. Our meeting was heavy with emotion, not knowing if we would ever see each other again, words inadequate.

But these meetings made the trip worthwhile. By the end of the year, with routine established, no social, physical or emotional demands, and despite a chest infection, I was getting back to how I was pre-trip.

Proud parents at Suhrud's graduation

* * *

Overwhelmed by grief, sadness, and the cumulative trauma of so many losses, I replace the handset on its cradle and let the tears flow. Seema is instantly at my side, wordlessly offering her support. Unnecessary to explain – the conversation had been brief, with few words from me, except for a hoarse, 'Thank you for telling me'. But I know she understands the blow that has been delivered.

Sharad had passed away suddenly, just as he had predicted, from a haemorrhage, as a result of side effects of his treatment. My parents were gone, now my dearest friend too. Words come unbidden to my mind. 'All my loved ones are going. I think it will be me next.' I'm not aware of speaking out loud, but as Seema stiffens beside me, I realise that, regrettably, I have. In the emotional roller coaster journey of our lives, this is a new low.

But Seema and the children still depended on me. Needed me. I draw her to me. 'Don't worry, we have faced all our troubles together. We will face this too. I will not abandon you.'

* * *

Doctor's offices, with me on the patient's side of the desk, have become all too familiar a scene in the drama that is my life. In psychiatry we go for a more informal arrangement –- comfortable chairs placed as for a chat with friends. There is something almost confrontational about this arrangement: doctor on one side, patient on the other. A coldness in the bland, impersonal furnishings.

With my body failing me, maintaining hope and a positive mindset now demand every ounce of strength I possess. But

I am determined, for Seema's sake. For Ruchi and Suhrud.

In February, I was briefly admitted to hospital for an episode of amnesia and confusion. Tests showed no neurological cause. Earlier, November's appointment with the cardiologist had confirmed a deterioration in my condition, but nothing that justified my being moved to the urgent transplant list. It's now March, three years after the verdict that, without a transplant, I might have two or three years left. I attend clinic again, cautiously hopeful that perhaps this time I will be transferred to the urgent list.

Sitting behind his desk, the transplant consultant delivers the fatal prophecy: 'Dr Banhatti, as you know, you don't at present fulfil the criteria for inclusion on the urgent list.

'The combination of your blood group and height means that suitable hearts are rare. Any that do become available will always be offered to those on the urgent list first. I'm sorry Rajeev, but in the current circumstances, we can't offer any firm idea about when - or even whether - a heart might become available for you.'

I sit in front of him, stunned to silence.

After all the promises and the beautiful picture that has been painted about how my transplant will happen, am I now to be denied any possibility of a new heart?

He then proceeds to explain that, because of the condition of my kidneys, they may even take me off the transplant list.

The irony of it appears to evade him: my heart is not bad enough to justify my inclusion on the urgent list, only bad enough that my other organs are failing for lack of blood. If, in some mythical future, I am reassessed as needing continuous inpatient treatment to keep me alive, I will become eligible for the urgent list, but it will likely be too late, as I will be unfit for surgery. I have been consigned to a scrap heap to wither away and die.

I feel as though I've been thrown into a deep, dark well.

Thoughts and questions whirl as he continues to talk, when another mention of the routine list snaps me back to the present. Did he really just say there is no routine list?

I become aware of Seema, weeping beside me, and my wife's distress pierces my soul. What would happen to her if I died? In a rush, my resolution returns. It's time to take my fate into my own hands. We leave the consultant's room in a state of confusion at his pronouncements, but gathering my wits, once home, I go into action.

I make calls to colleagues in India: 'What would be the possibility of getting the needed transplant abroad?' The answers are not encouraging. It could be done, but at a potential cost of millions. I research international guidelines for transplant patients and discover that I fulfil all the criteria. I write to my doctors at the transplant centre:

Dear Dr _

Re: Appt on 13/03/2014

I attended the appointment at _ Hospital along with my wife, Seema Banhatti. Dr _ performed the right-sided cardiac catheter test and then we saw Dr _.

We were left in a state of lack of clarity about my future care after the appointment. Indeed, it was quite confusing to hear some things which did not make sense from our point of view and since my life may literally depend on decisions being made about me we thought it is important to seek clarity regarding where I stand as far as getting a transplant at this hospital is concerned. We saw Dr _ today, who also would like clarity about what's happening.

In very brief, we were initially told that there are two lists, an urgent one and a routine one. I was on the routine one (for about 18 months) but there was no chance of getting a heart while I was on this as my blood group and height made it difficult to get a heart for me. In the rare instance a heart was found that was suitable for me, it would go to someone on the urgent list. We were told that there was no chance of getting a transplant while I was on the routine list, but I also do not fulfil the national and international criteria for the urgent list. This sounds like I am being consigned to a heap to wither away and die slowly!

This was the first time my height had been mentioned as a factor in deciding yes/no for a match. (Later I looked up the study and Johns Hopkins's criteria for eligibility, which are all fulfilled by me. A professor also states that height should never be the reason to refuse a heart; as often an optimum match may not be possible, but can be the difference between life and death!)

In the meantime I could not even tell about my worsening symptoms, which are:

1) Extremely dry skin leading to various eczema-like skin lesions, itchy rashes and increasingly varicose veins

2) An episode of TIA in 23/3/2014.

3) Insomnia, orthopnea, air hunger during night and severe cough, mucus.

4) Choking episodes and voice change. I am given to understand by Dr_ that, due to left atrial dilatation, there could be pressure over recurrent laryngeal nerve which explains the symptoms.

Then in the second part of the appointment we were told by Dr _ that actually there was no routine list and they just went ahead as a match became available. He said that I should not expect to get the call.

We saw Dr _ today but had little to say that clarifies the situation as we are still perplexed and a bit shocked. My wife had great faith in the system but now has lost it. Can you please write to clarify and copy it to Dr _ as per his request apart from my GP?

Please also send me or advise on accessing National/International criter-

> *ia for urgent list that Dr _ made a reference to. I fulfil _'s criteria and a few criteria of centres of international repute (Johns Hopkins, Cleveland Clinic) eligibility for heart transplant.*
>
> *No offence is meant by queries in this letter and the only intention is to seek clarity for us all (us, Dr _ and my GP) with regard to where we stand and whether there is any hope of getting a transplant at _ Hospital.*

* * *

A week later I receive a phone call from Dr _, who stands by the statements made at the March appointment and says Dr _ agrees with him. My heart sinks. But there is hope: 'We'll see how things are in two months. If the objective indicators – to be clear, not your symptoms – are worse, we'll likely admit you for treatment, which will make you eligible for the urgent list.'

I write to the cardiologist at my local hospital:

> *Hello D_,*
>
> *Dr _ contacted me yesterday and we spoke for 15 min or so. He had received my letter. I also told him that I had a copy of his clinic letter. He explained the same things again. Then on query from me he explained that national criteria to do it urgently are: 1)someone having a non-functional heart after acute event e.g., infarct, 2)Someone that has to be on two drugs (usually in hospital) which are essential for prolonging life. This is the dopamine iv that Dr _ had mentioned in November and Seema had to remind of it to Dr _. 3) Then he mentioned clinical discretion being the third when they will circulate the history to the UK group (which has a chairperson) and then do it urgently.*
>
> *2 or 3 may apply to me in future but then I should be transplantable candidate when that happens. Seema and I feel that we may already be there.*
>
> *We then discussed doing it in US, Spain, France or Germany. Spain apparently*

33

has a hospital where there is the biggest availability of hearts in Europe. After going thru this and second opinion he suggested that personally he thinks I should see what happens in 2 months as it's likely that they will admit me for treat-ment if objective indicators (not symptoms) are worse. He also said that he suppor-ted what Dr _ said in Nov and also Dr _ supported him (I suppose in not putting me on urgent list on 13th March). So while its a bit reassuring I am none the wiser. Waiting for follow up at present unless something changes clinically. Leaving it to fate and keeping positive expectation of eventual outcome!

Regards
Rajeev

∗ ∗ ∗

What to think? There is a glimmer of hope that in two months I may be transferred to the urgent list, but also dread and fear that the condition of my kidneys may prevent the operation.

For the next two months, it's hard to focus on anything but the next appointment. I try to distract myself with writing my blog, listening to music and audio books, and drawing inspir-ation from Buddhist philosophy. Seema ensures my nutrient intake remains adequate. Her quiet presence is a constant re-assurance.

Eventually, 21st May arrives. There are the usual tests; then I find myself once again facing a member of the transplant team on the opposite side of a desk. It's a different doctor this time – a man of great compassion. Every muscle in my body is tense. My very existence may depend upon this con-versation. The doctor pauses, then says the words that, after all this time, possess something of the quality of a magical formula: 'I'm recommending that we admit you early next week for diuretic therapy and probably inotropic therapy. You will be in hospital now until we can find you a heart.'

After so long waiting it's hard to take in, but I manage, 'Thank you Doctor, thank you so much'.

* * *

From the transplant consultant to my GP, 23rd May 2014:

Dear Dr _

re: Dr. Rajeev Banhatti (b. 23.9.60),

<u>Diagnosis:</u>
1. Idiopathic Restrictive Cardiomyopathy
2. NYHA Class Ill
3. Atrial tachy-arrythmias with multiple ablation procedures
4. Minor coronary artery disease 2001

I saw Rajeev on the 21 May 2014. He has deteriorated significantly since I last saw him and looked extremely unwell. He cannot walk more that about fifty feet without pausing and walks very slowly. In his wife's words 'he has aged thirty years'.

His weight was 88.6 kilograms. Blood pressure 102/70 mm.Hg. Jugular venous pressure was raised to the angle of the mandible. He had marked peripheral oedema and pulsatile hepatomegaly. A third heart sound was audible. He has folliculitis for which Tetracycline has been advised.

Chest x-ray showed cardiomegaly with perhaps a small right pleural effusion but there was no significant change compared to one done two months ago.

Electrocardiogram showed atrial flutter with a ventricular rate of 80 per minute.

<u>Current Medication</u>
Torasemide 40 mg daily
Metolazone 2.5 mg once a week Bisoprolol 1.25 mg daily Allopurinol 300 mg daily
Warfarin as per INR

Gaviscon Advanced as required

<u>Investigations</u>
Haemoglobin 119 g/litre: white cell count 5.2: platelets 84
C-Reactive Protein 2
Sodium 138: potassium 3.9: urea 23.0: creatinine 143: eGFR 48
INR2.5 Albumin 29: bilirubin 34: ALT 97: alkaline phosphatase 184

<u>Right Heart Catheterisation</u>
Right atrial pressure mean of 27 V wave up to 31
Right ventricle 58/28
Pulmonary artery 57/27 mean of 40
Pulmonary capillary wedge pressure mean of 30 V wave up to 40
-   Pulmonary artery saturation 49%
-   Cardiac output 4.9 litres/minute with an index of 2.4
By the Fick method 3.4 with an index of 1. 7
-   Transpulmonary pressure gradient 10 mm.Hg.
Pulmonary vascular resistance 3.0 Wood Units

<u>Management</u>
I have arranged to admit him to hospital early next week for a period of intravenous diureses and perhaps inotropic therapy. He is grossly fluid overloaded, his dry weight likely to be well below 80 kilograms. He has evidence of impaired renal and liver function with the fluid overload, it is possible that we may need to keep him in hospital until transplantation is feasible.

I email the cardiologist at my local hospital again:

*Hello D_*

I saw Dr _ on 21st May. Cardiac cath was also done. He advised me to come in for intravenous treatment and to stay until a transplant is done. He thought that I had worsened too much since Nov when he saw me. Though this is what we wanted, coping with it now that I have to go in on Tuesday (27th) is a big process. Will keep you updated.

I later wrote in my diary: '*Another physician saw me for a second opinion and was aghast at how I was dealt with and admitted me. In spite of all this, a transplant was in a distant and uncertain future.*'

Chapter Three

Transplant

Musings

'There is no such thing as a free lunch'. Before that thing called existence came into being there was only perfection. But perfection does not experience its own existence, so somehow there is a desire to know itself. But desiring something means being imperfect, as perfection has no deficit anywhere.

So the desire, like a ripple on the once-still ocean, gives rise to more ripples, as the movement of a ripple is only possible by pushing still water into another ripple. And so on.

These ripples travel further and further away but still have a direct connection to the origin. So consciousness is associated with space and time, self/non-self, life and death, like and do-not-like. Breaking this chain by replacing ignorance with wisdom, leading to nirvana, means becoming something where the concept of becoming and non-becoming do not arise. Maybe going somewhere before the singularity ever took place anywhere.

I was admitted on 3rd June 2014. Following the usual formalities, the consultant wasted no time in getting me on three types of diuretics to reduce the load of fluid I carried.

The diuretic therapy relieved my body of thirteen surplus

litres of water – thirteen kilos of extra weight I'd been carrying around with me. I was also put on the dopamine drip, the missing eligibility criterion for the urgent transplant list.

Physically I was weak, psychologically, a mass of conflicting emotions: hope that I was at last on the final length of my journey, fear that I would not get a new heart in time. But my psychological needs were cared for as well as my physical needs. The old campus of the transplant hospital offered a sense of security and inspired confidence. We both felt surrounded by a blanket of warmth and kindness.

I remember the legendary black swan that lived in the pond in the grounds. Patients were allowed to visit this peaceful place in a wheelchair. The black swan is a symbol of transformation and growth. It also represents the dark side of things, the unknown or hidden aspects, and in some cultures it is seen as a symbol of rebirth and renewal. At that time, we really did not know what lay ahead of us and it seemed to convey that.

Seema remained alongside me, her usual steadfast presence. But, after the diuretic treatment, shock and worry were plain in her face when she saw my legs – two brown, dried up wooden trunks. No muscle, no fat. Just skin and bones. I was now alive only because of the dopamine drip; no-one could know when a donor heart would become available. Admitting me, the consultant had said, 'We can do everything else, but you must pray for a heart.' The uncertainty continued.

So did the complications; I lost a lot of blood after a tooth extraction, upsetting the balance of electrolytes. An assessment by a Speech and Language therapist revealed that my swallowing problem was due to weakness of the muscles involved, caused by the low output from my heart. I could no longer walk and the condition of my kidneys necessitated a catheter and a urine bag. The catheterisation led to a stay in ICU . . .

It's afternoon on the ward. Seema is reading me the news from India when the nurse comes to change my catheter. As Seema continues to read, I begin to feel remote, as though viewing a scene in a dream. I'm red hot, shivering violently. Then nothing, until I wake in ICU, attached to a drip containing intravenous antibiotics for a urinary infection. Seema sits beside me, her eyes full of anxiety.

It had been a terrifying experience for her, powerless to act as my blood pressure started dropping. And – as she thought – watching me die in front of her. The cardiologist reassured her with his usual calm confidence: 'Don't worry, these things happen. A couple of days in ICU and he'll be back on the ward.'

I was in a top class hospital with scrupulous hygiene, but my weakened immune system made me vulnerable to such infections. The staff's quick action meant I was treated promptly and effectively and the cardiologist's prediction of my being back on the ward in a couple of days proved correct. But that day Seema was convinced she was losing me. Another terrifying rock-bottom moment in the emotional roller coaster of my heart transplant journey.

She later told me that, for the three months I waited in hospital for a heart, she would return to our empty home each evening, wondering when – or if – I would ever see it again. I wasn't the only one living with uncertainty.

* * *

Days turned to weeks, weeks to months. I had waited so long to be classed as an appropriate candidate for transplant. Was I to die now, at the final hurdle? My cardiologist's calm confidence helped both me and Seema immeasurably. He wasn't alone. The care provided by the transplant centre went far beyond the medical. From nurses, constantly on the go for their eight-hour shifts, but always available to encourage, comfort, and answer questions – to doctors, occupational therapists and the many other professionals who cared for me. No matter how busy, they were always happy to set our minds at rest with explanations of what was happening.

Medical people are as human as any. I know I've met a few who weren't as sensitive or conscientious as one would hope. But overall, the staff were unfailingly professional, always approachable and responsive to our questions and concerns. This transparency and openness fostered trust and confidence among patients and relatives alike.

And I wasn't always the easiest of patients – getting fractious as the anaesthetic wore off following the tooth extraction. Calling the nurse over and over, convinced she wasn't looking after me properly. Sending bloody pictures of myself to Seema at home to get her to complain to the hospital. Or grumbling loudly about the consultant on his rounds, accompanied by a group of students. 'Seema – you must complain to PALS' (the Patient Advice and Liaison Service).

The transplant team understand the enormity of what their patients face and don't overreact. I later apologised to that consultant, and was humbled when my apology was greeted with good humour and compassion.

* * *

I was in a nightmare world of pain, discomfort, and anxiety for my future. Two and a half years of the increasing certainty of an untimely death unless a new heart was found. Of doing my best to stay positive and maintain the ordinary activities of life. Driving to work every day despite my deteriorating condition; providing the best possible care for the troubled young people I worked with; being a loving husband and father. Trying not to let my illness spoil the small pleasures – good food, music, the company of friends and family. Not to let my struggles get in the way. Trying to retain a sense of humour. To be strong for them.

A lifetime of taking a philosophical approach to life and the insights I had gained from meditation and Buddhist teachings sustained me through those years. I had learned it was better to accept my fate and deal with it, rather than battling it. To passionately live every day – the ordinary and the extraordinary. To appreciate the good things life brought.

But as I lay in my hospital bed, I knew that, without a new heart, my time was short. I clung to anything that resembled normality. Including the normality of Seema just being there. I could be demanding of her as well as my doctors:

'Rajeev, I can't come tomorrow.'

'Why?'

This conversation played out several times as, in my private world of pain, fear and exhaustion I lost sight of the heavy burden she bore: three months of the daily fifty-mile round trip to visit me, with very little time left for herself, having already given up working so we could spend the time together, and doing all the driving in the years when I was deteriorating. To say nothing of the emotional toll those painful years of waiting exacted on her.

I felt, and feel, immense gratitude for the care I received, for having such a loving, supportive family who never once complained about the impact of my illness on their lives. They went to enormous lengths to make possible two things for which I will forever be grateful.

* * *

I'd been missing our dog, Leo, and leaving the hospital staff in no doubt about how much. In the end, the doctor said to

The legendary black swan and peaceful pond in the hospital grounds

The day Leo came to see me in hospital

Seema, 'Okay, you can bring the dog. He won't be allowed in, but Rajeev can go out.' So, complete with drip, I arrived at the back door, in a wheelchair. There, Ruchi met me for a few precious minutes with Leo. It was an experience of light and joy at a dark time. But that was nothing compared to the effort required to get me to my daughter's wedding.

* * *

Ruchi and Alex's wedding was set for 20th July 2014. Seema had moved mountains to ensure that everything was ready on the day: venue, caterers and photographer booked, chairs hired, guests invited, accommodation arranged. The mehndi ceremony was to be at home the evening before. On the great day the civil wedding and traditional Hindu ceremony would take place at the hotel, with a dinner and reception the same evening.

It gave me great sadness not to be more involved in the preparations, but there was one task I could help with, even from a hospital bed; I'm not sure if the manager of Majestic Wine had ever agreed the wine selection for a wedding reception by mobile phone with a hospital patient before! But my clothes were ready, my speech written.

Despite being in terminal condition and extremely weak, I had been given special permission to attend the ceremony – complete with catheter and drip. The consultant helped Seema to arrange a private ambulance with two specialist paramedics and a private nurse. Looking back, it's hard to believe it really happened.

The morning before, Ruchi phoned me. She was worried – they'd been forecasting hail for the 20th of July for weeks. I was encouraging: 'Don't worry. Be positive. It will be sunny.'

And so it was. The predicted hailstorm arrived the day before. Against all the odds, Ruchi's big day was gloriously sunny. On the morning of the 20th, a close friend who is an anaesthetist arrived to help me dress and travel with me in the ambulance, along with the medical team. It was a daunting prospect, leaving the safety of the hospital to brave the outside world. Thanks to the love and support of family, friends and medical professionals, and despite being in hospital with a terminal heart condition, I was there to fulfil my fatherly duty – and deep desire – and see my wonderful daughter marry the man she loves.

Proud parents again - this time at Ruchi's wedding

* * *

After everything I'd been through, when the moment I'd been waiting for so long arrived, it was strange that I was almost devoid of emotion . . .

23rd July 2014, three days after the wedding. I'm utterly drained, but still basking in the joy of being able to play my part in my daughter's big day. Seema phones to let me know that all the guests have gone home and she will come to visit today. Despite being exhausted, I'm looking forward to seeing my wife. An accident closes the road, and it's 5pm before she reaches the hospital. She stays until 10 pm, meaning she doesn't get home until nearly midnight. It's no surprise when she phones next morning to say she can't come today. Disappointing, but I understand.

In the middle of the night I wake from a fitful sleep – despite the painkillers and numerous other medications, I'm never really comfortable. Gradually, I become aware that someone is gently shaking my shoulder. 'Whaaa...?' I mumble. A whispered voice: 'Doctor Banhatti, can you wake up?' In the dim light from the nurses' station, I recognise one of the night nurses. 'I don't want to disturb the other patients. Can you sit up?' Still half awake, I try to take in the anaesthetist's words: 'I'm sorry to disturb you, Dr Banhatti, but there's a possibility we may have a new heart for you today. The donor team have already left to collect it, and assuming the tissue match is good, we'll start the operation at six o'clock. So we need to get you prepared for theatre just in case. I'll be back a bit later to let you know.'

I should be excited, or nervous. But I am oddly calm. Maybe it's shock. I realise that it's all been going on so long, I had stopped believing in the reality of a transplant for me. Now the moment is here, all I feel is a kind of acceptance of my fate. I will live or die; there is nothing more I can do.

The nurse is talking, and it dawns on me that she's been speaking for several minutes. ' ..., so would you like to phone her now?'

'Oh … um …What time is it?'

'Half past midnight.'

Poor Seema. A ringing phone at night will make her think the worst. But the nurse is right – she will want to be here, and it's better if she has some warning. The phone rings and rings, and when she answers, I can hear the anxiety in her voice. 'Rajeev?' In a moment of insight, I understand how much she has suffered these last years. The strange lack of emotional affect I'm experiencing allows me to explain what is to happen, and reassure her.

Around two, I phone again. 'The anaesthetist says everything is fine. They're going ahead with the operation, so a nurse is coming to get me ready. I will go to theatre at six am and it will take six and a half hours. I want you just not to worry. Just get up and have a cup of tea and be here at seven. You can come and wait in the waiting room outside the operating theatre.'

* * *

This is my memory of the transplant operation, which I wrote in my diary sometime later:

I remember my hospital trolley going through a double door – 'Operation Theatres', or something like that. A lady in a bright yellow saree doing a namaskar (traditional Indian greeting) or saying, 'Hi, I am Doctor _. I will be operating', or 'I am your surgeon.' And something to the effect of 'it will be alright', but definitely with a pleasant smile.

Then I have a very faint recollection of someone, a nurse, I think, telling me something and very soon losing consciousness.

Then I strongly remember a spell during which I seemed to be trav-

elling through a dark space though having some awareness of my body being horizontal. After God knows how long I suddenly remember seeing Baba, with his glasses on, and Aaee. They both are sitting on a bench, or two chairs, close by and looking down at me, though at my body rather than my eyes. Then Baba gets up a bit, looks intently and is a bit serious. Then he has a slight relieved smile as he sits down and whispers something in Aaee's ears getting closer to her. She also displays the same smile.

While this is going on I am suddenly aware of a slinky, rubbery, lardlike, shining, simmering at times, criss-cross pattern all around, as if the universe is made up of this mesh-like appearing/disappearing, chimera/mirage-like structure. Suddenly some woman-like being, like a mermaid — no legs — appears to travel fast up and down. Appearing and disappearing very fast for less than a split second. I feel it's Mimmi (my late mother-in-law) and she is a bit restless, trying for something. Then it all disappears and before, or after, all this I keep travelling through space.

I want to try and remember the face and name of Swami Samarth, but cannot. I also remember thinking about Sharad (my best friend who died suddenly six months before the op), and not finding him, but just feeling his presence as an intimation of him being present everywhere and nowhere if that can make sense. Then I am unable to fully recall the face of Swami Samarth but feel a frightening urge to recall it, as if my life (going back to earth) was dependent on it.

I still don't recall how clearly I remembered the face, but with a sudden flash of golden yellow lightning like a light bulb, I am back to the land of the living and aware of, first Suhrud, and then Seema by my bedside in the hospital looking down at me.

* * *

For three days after the operation I was in a coma, a harrowing experience for Seema and the children. This is her account of that time:

On the morning of 25th July, I was up early. I hadn't been able to sleep much after 2.30 am anyway, after Rajeev confirmed that they were going to take him to the operating theatre at 6 am. Finally, the moment we'd been waiting for had arrived. Those two and a half years had felt like an eternity. On the phone, he had told me they would take him in at six o'clock, and the operation would take six to six and a half hours. Not to hurry. To be here by 7 am and wait in the relatives waiting room outside the Critical Care Unit (CCU). Someone would come and inform me.

Somehow, I felt calm and positive and did as I was told. I was very confident that he was in the best place and being looked after in the best way possible. There were a couple of other families in the waiting room whose loved ones were fighting for their lives too. We were all trying to be strong and brave for each other, knowing exactly what each of us was going through.

At 12.30, Rajeev's cardiologist and his cardiac surgeon came over. They both greeted me and told me that, as far as they were concerned, the operation had gone well. Rajeev was in a medically-induced coma. They said he would be brought to the CCU by 2.30 pm and I was welcome to go in and sit by his side when they tried to wake him up. They also warned me that he might not wake up on the first attempt, as the body has undergone a huge procedure. I was relieved. He was out of the theatre with a new heart. At the same time, there was sadness in my heart too - for the donor's family, for what they must be going through.

On that first day, the doctors were weaning Rajeev off the powerful anaesthetics and attempted to wake him up at 2.30 pm. Rajeev had his eyes rolled up towards the sky, trying to open them but struggling to come out of the coma. They tried for a few minutes and realised he wasn't going to come around. I had crossed my fingers and was hoping he would. Gently, the cardiologist told me, 'Seema, Rajeev is not waking up. It can happen; the body undergoes a shock and sometimes requires longer. We will try again tomorrow. The CCU nurses are very competent. They will keep looking after him. You go home and come back tomorrow.' That kindness and support somehow gives you all the strength you need. I don't know how I drove home, tears flowing all the way. I called family in India, informed my friends that the operation had taken place. I had my son and our fur-baby Leo at home. My daughter was anxious on the other end of the phone too. I had to be strong for my children. I told them their Baba will wake up the next day.

Day 2. I went to CCU. The intensivist and cardiologist were ready to wake him up again in the CCU. Rajeev was still in a coma. They tried to wake him up. The anaesthetics had been reduced earlier in the day. They tried calling his name. Again, I could see Rajeev's eyes just rolling skywards as he lay on his hospital bed with multiple tubes and needles attached to all parts of his body. I could see just the whites of his eyes. I was praying hard for a miracle. I called out his name many times. The cardiologist looked at me. He knew I was nervous and afraid. He was calm. He spoke in a gentle voice, repeating the same words. He said, 'Rajeev is tired after the big operation. Every person is unique, and the body reacts differently. Let him rest. We will try to wake him up again tomorrow.' I was at the end of my tether. I just nodded, feeling numb.

I sat in the waiting room for a few hours. Those two other families were going through the same turmoil. An elderly gentleman was waiting for news on his wife, and a mother and daughter-in-law were anxiously awaiting news on their son/husband. We consoled each other. Being with them, I felt I wasn't alone. When there was no change after a few hours, I drove home. I called Ruchi, and we both cried over the phone, not knowing what was going to happen.

Day 3. That day Suhrud accompanied me to the hospital. Maybe somehow he knew his mum needed some extra strength. I had complete faith in Rajeev's cardiologist. I still believed Rajeev was in the best possible hands and in the best place, and hoped for miracles. A gem of a man like Rajeev, who never wished anyone ill, devoted son, loving father and amazing husband who was loved by everyone, had to survive. He just had to. The cardiologist and the intensivist came to the CCU.

It must have been just before lunchtime. Rajeev was still surrounded by multiple tubes attached to different machines. The CCU nurses were there twenty-four hours a day, watching, monitoring each and every number on those screens. They tried waking him up - calling his name, holding his hand. I was afraid, but Suhrud held my hand, and we both watched Rajeev's face intently for any sign. The eyes were moving up and down. He was making an effort. Next moment, he opened his eyes, and the first thing he saw was Suhrud.

The cardiologist was happy, checking all the numbers on the screen, making sure all the parameters were satisfactory. Rajeev was still groggy and could not speak, but even in that state, with all those tubes, his eyes flickered with recognition and spoke volumes. We were all just stunned to witness such a miracle.

* * *

Waking from the coma was only the beginning. The surgeon and the cardiologist were both happy with how the operation had gone. However, there were many trials to be overcome. On the fourth day, my exhausted kidneys began shutting down, and I was put on a kidney machine. Then, as my lungs struggled to fully open, a tracheostomy was needed – the procedure where a hole is made in one's windpipe, allowing oxygen to be supplied direct to the lungs. A procedure that's unpleasant, uncomfortable, and prevents the patient from speaking.

I was still delirious, and having hallucinations due to the morphine. Seema gave me a notepad so I could write what I wanted to say, but what looked like writing to me was – to everyone else – just scribble. It was a waking nightmare – seeing cars on the roofs of the buildings outside and other strange things around me. Trying desperately to communicate to my uncomprehending family and medical staff. In the end, an occupational therapist brought in an alphabet chart with letters I could point to. This was incredibly laborious, but did at least allow some communication. Combined with the indignity of not having control of one's bowels, those early days were hell.

But the care was first class – nurses checking my bloods every four hours, and the consultant dropping in four or five times a day, reviewing the effect of every little change in medication. The nurses seemed to have endless supplies of patience and cared for me with great compassion, providing constant reassurance to Seema, too.

* * *

I was weaned off the kidney machine. Ten days after the operation, I was moved out of ICU, first into a side room and then onto the ward for nearly a month. It was a challenging, sometimes depressing, time: trying to maintain my dignity as I discovered I couldn't remember how to use a mobile phone, knowing that my loyal Seema was doing her best to prompt me without making it obvious. Bringing me books of word jumbles to keep me occupied and help get my brain working again.

The first time I tried to stand up from a chair, disaster struck. As I pushed on the armrests for support, searing pain erupted in my chest as the stitches at the top of my sternum opened up. Yet another procedure to dry off the wound. Still, as a result, Seema asked for the occupational therapist to come and see me. She at once arranged for higher chairs in the ward, benefitting everyone.

There were other, more serious, setbacks. Our immune systems treat transplanted organs as foreign bodies and attempt to destroy them – rejection. This response is controlled by drugs that heavily suppress the immune response; transplantees have to take them for the rest of their lives. The risk of rejection is greatest in the first year following transplant and I would have monthly biopsies to check whether my body was tolerating my new heart.

The first rejection came within weeks. After everything I'd been through, God was still trying me. The medical team treated it with their usual calm professionalism, using high doses of steroids. Then an anxious wait till the next biopsy – which, thankfully, was clear.

And my heart was working well. Bit by bit, I gained strength, and some of the problems caused by the lack of blood circulation resolved themselves. We take so much for granted – getting a drink of water, walking around our homes, eating a meal. Over the last two and a half years, my body had lost the ability to carry out these most basic functions, requiring constant medical intervention and the care of others just to keep me alive.

So imagine my elation when, a mere six weeks since my transplant, I celebrated my birthday with pizza! Very soon I would be back home with my family.

Second Time Around

Chapter Four

Rejections – the highs and lows, and getting back to work

I know emotions are often hard to describe as they are felt, especially the nuances and gradations of emotions, where desire, feelings and logically derived expectations intermingle.

They are like bubbles that break up before forming any meaningful gestalt.

12th September 2014: wearing my trusty grey fleece, I walk – unaided – through the front door of my home and come to a halt. So many months of wondering whether I would live to see this place again. I take in the familiar surroundings as if for the first time. Leo bounds up, tail wagging fiercely, and stops short, looking up at me in confusion. He's usually so vocal, but his surprise at seeing me after so long has silenced him!

We go into the lounge. When I was last in this room I was weak, emaciated, full of fear and uncertainty about my future. Now I have a future again. Seema fusses over me, telling me to sit down, fetching food and drink. Having got over his surprise, Leo is now super-excited. He snuggles up on my lap on the sofa, just like the old days. He too has been sick. Over the coming months, we will recover together, mutual comfort for each other.

I look around and take in the old familiar objects – ornaments and photographs, the pictures on the walls, my books and CDs, even the furniture on which I sit. I take in the warm, furry bundle that is Leo. Later I walk around the house, touching everything I see in wonder. In awe of their, and my, continued existence. Seema follows me, solicitous. I know she is exhausted from the months of travelling daily to be at my side during my long stay in hospital. Our eyes meet and I realise she is weeping. Tears prick my own eyes in a tender moment of mutual understanding.

The next morning, we share the luxury of the first cup of tea together. The simple act of drinking tea is transformed from the satisfying of a physical need into an act of tremendous significance. Every sensation heightened – the aroma of the tea, the warmth of the cup, the flavour of the drink on my tongue. The sitting here at our kitchen table. Just being alive has become something remarkable. From this time on, I will live every day of my life. Appreciate it. Never again will I take anything for granted.

The road to recovery will be long. My body, weakened by the years of inadequate blood supply and major surgery, needs good food, physiotherapy and rehabilitation to regain its strength, as well as the immunosuppressants I will need for the rest of my life. For the first year the risk of rejection is acute, and it will take time to arrive at an optimum combination of the drugs to control this. We have been warned that these medications, though necessary, are very strong and there are side effects.

But for now, the overriding emotion is a quiet sense of joy. At being alive. At being here for my dear wife and children. But I can't help a sense of guilt too – that our happiness has come at the cost of someone else's misery. One day I will write a letter of thanks to my donor's family. Not now – the emotions are too raw. But I know that, one day, the time will be right.

* * *

Once again, we sit in the cardiologist's consulting room. 'The biopsy shows a rejection – 2R – not the most severe but we do need to treat it'. My new heart pounds. No words come. I can sense Seema's tension as she sits beside me.

Will this state of constant uncertainty about my future ever end? It's November 2014, three months since my op, and my body is rejecting its new heart for the second time. Is this a sign? We have, after all, met other patients who had no rejections.

'There's no need to worry. We'll bring you in for a couple of days, and treat it intravenously with steroids, then gradually reduce the dose with tablets. And we still have plenty of weapons in our armoury.'

The cardiologist listens carefully to our questions about the treatment and answers equally carefully. My respect for this compassionate man is immense. He reassures us that this is only a setback, not a death sentence.

I pull myself together. Yes, Rajeev, attachment to a particular outcome only creates more suffering. When we accept what is happening and realise that facing is the only option, there is no rebellion or other option, it becomes easier.

I reach over to shake his hand. 'Thank you so much Doctor, I have great confidence in you.'

A month later, the biopsy shows no rejection. There is the 'little' problem of a dose of flu, but I am recovering, and we breathe easy again for a while.

* * *

New Year's Eve 2014. What a difference between this day and one year ago! Hardly able to walk, or even eat. My professional life over. Not knowing whether I would still be here to celebrate in a year's time.

I am the star attraction at our traditional New Year celebration with old friends – no-one else has a new heart! Ruchi and Alex are here too, their first New Year as Mr and Mrs Cross. We settle in for an evening of convivial conversation and enjoying some delicious foods. 'Come,' I say, opening the bottle of Johnny Walker Blue Label Whiskey I had been saving for the wedding, 'This was meant for sharing.'

I begin the familiar ritual, 'Swirl it in the glass … breathe in the aroma … What can you smell? … Take a sip… slowly now … What do you think? …'

Such joy to embrace the delights of sharing food and drink with loved ones once again. To bite off a morsel of food, to taste and swallow.

It is a bittersweet pleasure though. The lingering feelings of guilt and sorrow that our joy depends on another family's heartache never leave me. But I am here! Here for Seema and for my children. My gratitude is so great it's almost too much for my new heart to contain.

Later in January, my biopsy shows a third rejection. This time it's treated with immunoglobulin – antibodies. One of the immunosuppressants is reduced, and another introduced.

We try to stay calm. We are upset, but we have learnt that the best way to cope is by accepting what is happening and dealing with it, rather than being attached to things being a particular way. We carry on.

* * *

The following month my biopsy showed no rejection, and we breathed another sigh of relief, at the same time attempting to accept the good news as calmly as the bad; no need to increase our suffering by building up our hopes, only to have them dashed next month.

The repeated rejections meant physiotherapy had to wait; local reorganisation of rehabilitation services meant there was no rehab programme for me. I believe these two factors had a significant impact on the length and degree of my recovery.

I was still weak, and my capacity to undertake any substantial mental activity was limited. I had once been a master of multitasking. Now, even non-physical activities took a lot of energy. Self-knowledge was a boon. Understanding my inner workings allowed me to make a choice to work slowly and carefully.

Seema's support through these months of continuing uncertainty was unwavering. I was often so bound up in my own difficulties I didn't always fully express my gratitude at the time. But I would later write in my journal:

'How she must be suffering on many levels and keeping love, compassion and loyalty alive in the face of many conflicting emotions.

She has stood by me through thick and thin. She has spared no efforts in making sure that I am as comfortable as I can be. I am alive not only because of her, but for her and for my children. Whenever I pass on, they should know that I was a completely satisfied and happy person.

Happy husband, man and father.'

23rd March 2015. I am again sitting in the cardiologist's office hearing that my new heart has been rejected. He feels I won't respond to immunoglobulin again, but there is a research level drug called Campath (Cambridge Pathology Laboratory), which he thinks my body will respond to. Acquiring it involves mountains of paperwork and a high cost – £10,000 for one ampoule. So I wait patiently for everything to go through. It will be infused via a saline drip over a certain period of time.

* * *

It was an anxious day for Seema; I will let her tell her own story:

We got there in the morning. They set up the drip, but then Rajeev was having effects like chemotherapy – nausea and vomiting. So they had to stop it for a while. Then the consultant said if we put it on a very slow speed he might tolerate it better, and that worked because I said, 'He has to.' Because he was doing it for us. The consultant just looked at me and smiled because I said he has to. The two consultants looked at each other and looked at me and Rajeev, and they said, 'Okay'.

At lunchtime they said, 'We'll take the drip off for a while, because that will give him a break. We'll take an hour's break.' The nurse who had taken the drip off went for lunch and didn't come for an hour and a half! I was getting restless and tried to call someone but get her back. Because I knew it had to be finished within a certain time. Luckily she came back and put it back on and it was finished in time.

Next time I visited the ward, they said 'Yes, you were the anxious one!' And I said, 'Of course I was anxious!' But after that, the next biopsy showed no rejection. So he was lucky.

* * *

I didn't know then, but this was to be the last rejection episode, so I was indeed lucky. In May, we had a delightful family holiday in a cottage in Devon. Unknown to any of us that week, another side effect of my treatment had begun its gradual unfolding.

* * *

From my journal:

After surviving rejections and brief hospital stays for acute rejections, in June 2015, I developed an organic confusional state with manic delusional symptoms and some hallucinatory experiences.

This state was brought on by the high doses of steroids used to counteract my body's rejection of its donor heart. It was a frightening episode, at the time known only to family and a very few close friends, an unusual psychological side effect of the medication that even many doctors were unaware of, and for which we were totally unprepared.

I experienced what seemed like a heightened state of awareness where I was capable of thinking at a super-fast speed, while also being aware that all was not well, and desperately trying to explain what was happening to my loved ones. I later wrote the following about my experience:

The Sound of Silence

I once experienced the sound of silence. It was a mind-state where I could actually think so fast to the exclusion of distracting stimuli, that I could experience and appreciate the space between two consecutive thoughts without any effort.

It's a precious but also scary dimension of experience where you exactly experience/understand psychotic mental processes. I think I did, but only to a certain extent, as I accept that people do experience and act out much more (worse, scarier, long lasting).

I am now unwilling to enter that dimension, but I know it exists. I have been to a mind state when all doubts about the other planes of existence, Buddhist sunyata doctrine, anittya, anatta, etc, were removed fully.

Looking back, the episode was a brutal encounter with the other side of the psychiatrist/patient relationship, and the need for compassion on the part of we doctors. I felt vulnerable and scared, wondering if I would recover, if my family would be able to cope if I didn't. It was also a test of my family's loyalty and resilience. They didn't let me down. Seema never wavered and in their turn, our children were her strength and support during that time.

* * *

25th July 2015, the first anniversary of my heart transplant. My donated heart had been quietly supplying blood to my ravaged body for an entire year. Many of the symptoms I had previously suffered – breathlessness, fatigue, swollen legs, muscle wastage, difficulty swallowing, and lack of mobility – were banished, hopefully for good. July's biopsy was the third in a row to be clear of rejection. It should have been a day for celebration, but it was hard to shake off my negative frame of mind.

I was still recovering from the previous month's psychiatric episode and was suffering constant attacks of gout – a side effect of so many diuretics. Bad enough that Seema took me to my July appointment in a wheelchair. In May I wrote to my transplant consultant: '*I have been getting cramps in my fingers and gouty or arthritic pains in toes or metatarsal joints and also had severe pain in right thigh/hip for three days akin to a strain. My dexa scan is scheduled for 13 July but I have also kept my GP informed to see whether a scan of my legs/hip is necessary locally.*'

My new heart was keeping me alive, but what kind of life? There's an entry in my diary: '*In 2015, quite weak. What did I do?*' The answer was: 'Not a great deal', but as summer turned to autumn, I began to realise that I was turning a corner.

By November, there had been no further rejections. The transplant team added a third immunosuppressant to my cocktail of drugs, but there would be no more biopsies or major changes in my management from then on, unless I had symptoms of rejection. I was still on medication for the side effects of the steroids, but my mood was now more stable, and, although I didn't know it, that was the last of the serious side effects.

Little by little, the drama and traumas were becoming part of my past, and I began to plan again for the future.

* * *

September brought two auspicious events: Suhrud starting a Masters' in Sound Design at Edinburgh and a surprise fifty-fifth birthday party – an occasion that at one time I had feared

I would never see. Somehow Seema managed to keep the plans under wraps. On the day, she said, 'We haven't been to the Gurkha Restaurant in a while, let's go there for your birthday'.

After such a horrible two months in the summer, walking in to find fifty people waiting to wish me well gave my confidence a boost. Ruchi had organised a heart-shaped cake with an ECG line going through it, and me and Leo sitting on a sofa. I felt privileged and grateful to be the recipient of so much love and support.

My unique fifty-fifth birthday cake!

Next we visited Ruchi and Alex on Guernsey, taking Leo along on the ferry. It was a much-needed period of relaxation. I have beautiful memories of drinking the morning cup of tea with Seema, watching the sunrise.

I realised my physical condition no longer dominated my life, and began to consider the possibility of a return to work. In December, I applied to have my GMC licence to practise reinstated.

A trip to India in January 2016 was an opportunity to settle some family affairs and thank well-wishers who had prayed for me and kept our morale up through the nightmare years.

Prevented by the terms of my pension from being employed directly in the NHS, I set up a private limited company. This allowed me to work as a locum consultant, initially taking on contracts where I could travel from home, but gradually taking jobs further afield. I resumed offering workshops in Nagpur and attending conferences in Europe and India. I was offered the position of visiting faculty at NKP Salve Medical School, Nagpur. In 2016, I was selected to present a poster at the 15th Congress of the World Association for Infant Mental Health in Prague. It seemed that, not only had I cheated physical death, but somehow also risen from my professional death.

I took locum jobs further afield – Devon, Cornwall, Hull. These acquired a semi-holiday feel, as Seema would sometimes come and stay too. Everywhere there was kindness and warmth. My reputation often went ahead of me: 'Oh, you're that Dr Banhatti! I read your article in . . .'. Many of the patients I saw had been waiting two, three years for an appointment. I often felt guilty that I could only help a few, until someone pointed out to me that part of my role was to take responsibility for the whole team. Permanent staff brought their cases to me for review, advice and support; I felt valued. Later contracts took me to Jersey and the Isle of Man. I was engaged in what I loved doing. Being of service. I had long ago accepted my own mortality, but, strangely, my professional death was harder to bear, and I wanted to prove to myself that I was still the committed, conscientious doctor I aspired to be.

At the Prague conference

* * *

'Today I will do it.'

Seema's eyes light up at my words. She never says anything, but she had hoped I would write this letter long ago. 'What has changed, Rajeev?'

I sigh. In reality, I don't know. It's two years since my heart transplant. My new heart is working well, with the help of the immunosuppressants I'll be taking for the rest of my life. Life is good. Everything that was once denied me – work, holidays, enjoying time with family and friends, the ability to support those I love – is again mine. I've always intended to write a letter of thanks to the family of my donor, but somehow I just couldn't.

So many years of physical suffering, uncertainty, and roller coaster emotions. After everything I'd been through, it was hard to believe it was all over. To believe that my new heart would really solve the problems I had lived with for so long. And there was the guilt of knowing that for me to receive a heart, somebody else was no longer there. What can one say to a family whose misery has made possible one's own happiness? How to adequately express one's gratitude for being given a second chance at life? Images of the years of struggle – to breathe, to walk, to work, to enjoy life and be the husband and father I would wish to be – all these and more drift across my mind's eye.

'Rajeev, you're spilling your tea!'

We collapse into laughter, as Seema's words snap me out of my reverie, and she fetches a towel to mop up her inept husband.

Later that day, I go into my office, pull a sheet of paper from the packet on the shelf and sit down at my desk. I gaze out at our little garden for a few minutes and then start to write. Where, until then, there had been a blank, now words flowed onto the paper. Sealing the letter into its envelope, I feel lighter, relieved of a burden.

I never received a reply to my letter. One more reality I simply had to accept. Who knows what its recipients' feelings were, how welcome it was? Hard as it was for me to write, it was perhaps even harder for them to receive. As time went by, I came to understand that the best way of expressing my gratitude was by living my life to the full. By making good use of the second chance that had been so freely given.

* * *

Over the next few years, we took holidays in the US, Egypt, and Japan – where I did 20,000 steps a day, an unthinkable feat just a couple of years earlier. The trip to the US was to visit my cousin Bharat and an opportunity to express our gratitude to our dear friend, Veann, her husband Chris, who had supported and prayed for us during the nightmare years of my illness. Chris even postponed his own life-saving operations for our visit. There were visits to India to see family and friends and deliver workshops – giving back, fulfilling my purpose. Seema sometimes teased me about my desire to resume my professional life; I had always extolled the virtue of retiring early to enjoy my hobbies. But I felt so grateful for the life I had been given. From the time of my transplant, I resolved to live life, appreciating what I have and valuing every single day.

Just prior to the outbreak of coronavirus in the UK in 2020, we took a trip to Scandinavia, a kind of pilgrimage to the Wallander locations. Then another trip to Jersey, arriving back on the last flight before lockdown began and a further contract in the Isle of Man later in the year.

September brought a momentous occasion – my sixtieth birthday. Covid restrictions meant that, as for many others, it would be a quiet affair. In fact, I had thought that nothing was planned. But that morning Seema said to me, 'I think there's an email from Suhrud you should look at. Could you just check it?' Imagine my astonishment when I opened the message to find a video containing over seventy messages of good wishes for my birthday! Warm tears of happiness made their way down my cheeks as, one by one, those who meant most to me assured me of their continuing love and support. Ruchi had thought of it and Suhrud had been gathering the individual contributions and editing the entire piece for weeks. Six years after my transplant, I was blessed to have so many wonderful people in my life.

On holiday with Seema

Chapter Five

Transcendent Experience

When one becomes still in mind and body it is sometimes possible to experience what is described in the ancient Indian text, the Baghavad Gita, as 'Vishwaroopa', or 'seeing God in everything'. It is a state recognised by all the mystical traditions and cannot be fully explained, but only known experientially. I had my first spiritual experiences as a youth:

My brush with the divine

My first experience of losing my sense of being separate from my surroundings came in my childhood; this must be around fourteen years of age. I suspect I was sitting or lying down with my best friend on the terrace in Pachora. I looked up in the sky and said that the sky looked as if it was a big white balloon or bubble. I became a part of it and then I think I lost consciousness for a few seconds.

The second time was when I was in the second year of my

MBBS (Bachelor of Medicine, Bachelor of Surgery). I experienced depersonalisation and derealisation a few times and had a sense that something very meaningful was happening without knowing exactly what. I had a sudden idea that fate was not just blind chance. It was arranged or modified a bit by God. This God became a bald man who could rarely be seen, but he was very elusive and disappeared immediately even if you saw him.

(Journal, 16th October 2020)

I later experienced the sense of oneness during the ten day Vipassana Meditation course, and twice after touching Leo, a mystical or religious experience of oneness with all things. In his book 'Stillness Speaks', Eckhart Tolle describes it like this: 'Look at a tree, a flower, a plant. Let your awareness rest upon it. How still they are, how deeply rooted in "just being". Allow nature to teach you stillness. When you look at a tree and perceive its stillness, you become still yourself'.

This feeling of oneness has had a profound effect on me. When one feels such a deep sense of connection with everything else that exists, it inevitably leads to the desire for the wellbeing of all things, and the wish to harm nothing by one's actions. If one is fortunate, one may also receive deeper insights:

'Did I hear Lord Krishna laugh and show me the universe being born and destroyed?'

Chapter Six

Retirement bites

<table>
<tr><td>Ordinary
Achievement/Gains</td><td>Extraordinary
Achievements/Gains</td></tr>
<tr><td>Admission to medical school</td><td>Aaee, Baba</td></tr>
<tr><td>MBBS</td><td>Dilip-Radha, Ani-Manju</td></tr>
<tr><td>MD</td><td>Sushama, Pratibha, Nandu and Vrunda</td></tr>
<tr><td>MRC psych</td><td>Seema's parents</td></tr>
<tr><td>FRC psych</td><td>Reading</td></tr>
<tr><td>Examiner</td><td>My childhood friends</td></tr>
<tr><td>Tutor</td><td>Seema and children</td></tr>
<tr><td>International teaching and presentations/workshops</td><td>B J Medical school friends and close UK friends</td></tr>
<tr><td></td><td>Moments when enjoying music and concerts</td></tr>
<tr><td></td><td>All the holidays with family and friends</td></tr>
<tr><td></td><td>Brothers-in-law – Chaitanya, Sanjeev, Minesh</td></tr>
<tr><td></td><td>Sisters-in-law – Veena, Rajashree, Roopa</td></tr>
<tr><td></td><td>Close friends and family in India</td></tr>
<tr><td></td><td>Following cricket</td></tr>
<tr><td></td><td>Surprisingly LEO did not feature here till today (30/5/21)</td></tr>
</table>

2021: the world was still reeling from the chaos and fear of the coronavirus pandemic. Early in the year, the UK entered its third lockdown, followed by several months of constantly varying levels of restriction.

We enjoyed our stay on the Isle of Man in 2020 so much that I took another contract in the spring of 2021. But we were to discover again that sometimes life has other plans.

Just as our period of home quarantine was ending, Seema received news that her Dad needed to have a pacemaker fitted and decided to go and help care for him. When flights into the UK from India stopped in April, she was stuck there; as it turned out for five months! Our little family was spread across the world; Suhrud had been stuck in Japan since the beginning of the pandemic; now I was stuck in the Isle of Man, Seema in India, and Ruchi of course, in Guernsey.

* * *

Our family has been so long apart, we're desperate to see each other. As soon as foreign flights are allowed back into the UK, we ask Suhrud to come home for his birthday in August. It's agreed that he will arrive on the 1st; the rest of us will try to do the same. In the end, Seema has to wait until she is released from hotel quarantine on August 11th, but we are all excited at the prospect of being together again.

In the weeks prior to my leaving the Isle of Man, I notice the return symptoms of heart failure – breathlessness, fatigue, swollen feet. Is my body rejecting my donor heart again? I put aside these thoughts and focus on my return to Northampton.

'Are you sure you're alright to travel, Rajeev?'

'I'll be fine, don't you worry, I will be back in Northampton by this evening', I say, sounding more confident than I feel. 'I'm extremely grateful for your help with loading the car.' My

Isle of Man colleagues are solicitous – another example of the kindness and support that have made my two stays here such a pleasure.

'Thank you for being so understanding about my cutting this trip short. It's such a long time since our family has been together. I hope to be back again soon.'

As I speak, something tells me I may never return to the island, but I push the thought away. The previous evening, my nephew, who was working in Birmingham, had tried to persuade me to let him drive me home. 'It's no problem, Uncle Rajeev, I'm coming to see Suhrud, anyway.'

He is eager to help. It's what I would do for a favourite uncle, too. I pause. My breathlessness is making telephone conversations a little stilted.

'It's very good of you, but I think I'll give it a go.'

I can hear the concern in his voice as he answers, 'If you're sure, Uncle Rajeev. Don't forget, though. If you change your mind, even on the way, just ring me and I'll be there.'

By the time I turn off the M1 at Junction 15, I'm regretting my obstinacy. It's been a long, gruelling trip. The increased breathlessness and racing pulse of recent months make it hard to focus. Sitting in the driver's seat, my swollen legs feel like two tree trunks. For some reason my ankles have lost the up/down movement, making every gear change an enterprise fraught with risk in the heavy traffic. It seems much longer than the three hours the journey has taken.

It's a matter of minutes now, though, till I pull up outside our home in Northampton. I try to put aside the fear – a fear I have not yet confessed to Seema, stuck in India with no way to help – that my donor heart is failing.

I can't wait to see my family. These last months, separated from them, and anxious about my deteriorating health, have been an ordeal. Suhrud has already arrived and Ruchi and Alex should be there by now too. It will be several more days until Seema can join us, detained by the mandatory hotel quarantine. But this should be a joyous reunion and, despite my anxieties and the exhausting drive home, I'm in a celebratory mood.

And so it is. Hugs all round, all of us talking excitedly about our adventures. To save us the trouble of cooking after our long journeys, that evening we eat at a favourite restaurant. It is a merry occasion. From time to time I catch Ruchi looking at me, concern in her eyes. Later, when Alex and Suhrud are exchanging news of mutual friends, she presses me: 'You're not well, Baba. Why didn't you tell us?'

'Ah, dear Ruchi, you are so like your mother. I can't hide anything from you, can I? I didn't want to worry you. There was nothing you could do, after all.'

By the time Seema arrives, I am rested from my journey. But she is barely out of the car before she has taken in my breathlessness and difficulty walking. Bless her, she says nothing, just smiles sadly as we hug each other for the first time in months.

Later, when we are alone in our room, I explain: 'I have been in touch with the hospital. They want me to come in for a few days of investigations.' She draws a breath. 'I will come with you, but rest now, Rajeev.'

My heart swells with love and appreciation for the woman who has stood by me for so long. She never complains, but she has been through so much, always by my side.

I think back to that day, so many years ago, when we first met, two young people looking for a life companion. Both a bit awkward, unsure what to say. It might have been an arranged marriage, but it was not a forced marriage; we just asked for our families' help in finding a suitable wife or husband. The choice had been ours, and I had chosen well.

The next day, Suhrud tests positive for Covid, and I am banished to the spare room to avoid infection. The following day it's Seema who succumbs; Ruchi and Alex have escaped by leaving early. With Seema in self-isolation, it is my nephew who takes me to the transplant centre for three days of investigations in early September, on my sixty-first birthday.

* * *

Once again, we sit in an anonymous hospital consultation room opposite a cardiologist, waiting to hear the results of the investigations. What will this day hold? Is my body rejecting my donor heart, or is my donor heart now failing as my own did? When I began this journey, I was told a new heart might give me ten extra years. But is this the beginning of the end? I'm careful not to express these thoughts out loud.

'So, Rajeev, the good news is that there is no rejection of your heart. The tricuspid valve is weak, meaning your heart is working harder to prevent blood leaking back into the atrium. The high blood pressure you've been experiencing this year may also be causing pulmonary hypertension, leading to congestion around the heart.'

I look at Seema, who sits straight in her chair, hands in lap, attentive.

'We also looked into why your ankles are swollen. As you know, the pleura, which lines the chest cavity and surrounds the lungs, produces small amounts of lubricating fluid. Your body is producing excessive fluid – pleural effusion – and this is contributing to your breathlessness.

'There are things we can do – medications to help with the breathlessness and we can try a different diuretic which should reduce the swelling.'

Even as a qualified doctor, I'm finding it hard to follow the thread of the consultant's explanations. 'You mentioned a weak tricuspid valve. Can anything be done about that? Replacing the valve, for example?'

79

The doctor pauses, looks down at his papers, and then back up at me. 'I'm sorry, Rajeev, you're not fit enough for that kind of surgery any more. But there is a lot we can do to improve your symptoms'.

I come away with a prescription for increased diuretics and a measure of hope that this might resolve the breathlessness and swollen ankles.

Over the next three months, the swelling does reduce, improving my mobility, but my breathlessness remains unaffected.

* * *

December, my next appointment: 'There's a new drug that helps reduce breathlessness; it's a diuretic too, and has the fortunate side effect of removing excess blood sugar. Let's give it a try.'

On the way home, Seema is quiet. I reflect on our recent conversations with the consultant. I know that I'm on borrowed time. Eight years since my transplant. Eight years since I was told that, with a new heart, I might have ten years more.

My heart transplant journey had not been as smooth as some. The people we hear about are the ones who get straight back to the gym, climb mountains, run marathons. The long wait with a failing heart and resultant strain on my other organs. Four acute rejections in the first year, and the lack of physio and rehab – all this may all have affected the outcome for me.

Fear and uncertainty – my constant companions during the nightmare years – have been attempting a comeback in these last months. I've been ignoring their voices, not allowing them a hearing while there is still a chance. Not wanting to worry Seema.

It's becoming clear that there's never any mention of dealing with underlying causes, only symptom control. I've always known that I was on borrowed time, that eventually my donor heart would fail, as my own had done. I long ago came to terms with my own mortality. I must face the truth. If I am nearing the end, it is with sadness, but gratitude too.

There's an atmosphere between us as we pull off the motorway, a sense of something left unsaid. As Seema parks the car, neither of us moves to get out. She turns to look at me. Wordlessly, she offers her hand, her eyes full of pain, and it seems to me that there's an unspoken understanding. I know she will stand by me to the end.

* * *

I replace the phone in its cradle and I can't help the smile that spreads across my face. Seema comes through from where she's been sketching in her study, and I can tell she has guessed the content of the conversation.

'Guernsey?', she queries.

'Yes, my dear, we will go to Guernsey for three months.'

* * *

Following the realisation that I was now in a maintenance phase, symptom control only, I had decided it was time to give in gracefully, and retire. 'I enjoy my work, but my body is not supporting me. Only if someone asks me to take a locum in Guernsey.' I had been granted my wish.

It was a beautiful time. We rented an apartment, and I worked Monday to Thursday. Spending time with Ruchi and Alex. Watching the sun set over the sea.

I came home feeling calm. Eight years earlier, I had written in my blog:

When a naturally lazy man achieves a few academic degrees, works non-stop in a job for more than a couple of decades and fulfils obligations of Gruhasthashrama (in traditional Indian culture, the stage of married life), two things happen. One, he feels that finally he has earned the right to do nothing, and two, enjoying doing nothing is not too difficult for him.

When I look around and see people of similar ages who can retire as far as financial situation and other obligations are fulfilled, many of them appear unwilling to just follow their hobbies or enjoy life by just 'existing beautifully' (as Bertie Wooster would put it). No! They go looking for trouble by taking on a job or a business venture that they do not even seem to love or even like! Not for me, thank you! I would rather bear the guilt of being a 'time waster' and idler.

The first time I retired, I had ignored my own advice. This time I accepted it, I hope with grace. This time I would 'exist beautifully' and enjoy doing nothing but what pleased me. I was grateful, and I accepted.

* * *

Later in the year I realised I was missing Suhrud, who was still living in Japan. I said to Seema: 'Let's ask him to come home for a visit. It has been a year since he was here. Let's celebrate his 30th with a garden party. Spending time with my loved ones brings me happiness.' It was a joyous occasion with thirty or so close friends.

Chapter Seven

Giving up or letting go?

Giving up or letting go? It's difficult to think back to see what it was like at the time. I think it was both. There were days when I was able to let go of my fear of what will happen to others after I go. These others are simply three: Seema, Ruchi, Suhrud. I know Leo will be looked after as long as one of us four is alive. It is difficult just to describe the actual mindset or state of mind one experiences when one achieves the process of letting go. Difficult to re-attain that mind state even after having experienced it once.

I realise now that I had come to terms with my mortality before the transplant. Buddhism helped me a lot – 'anitya' (the Buddhist idea that everything passes – the things we like, as well as the things we don't like) became experientially palpable or experienceable as opposed to knowable or known by inference, thought and to some extent emotion. It is a good but 'difficult to describe' or attain experience to have that mind state where you have let go.

This has somehow made it quite difficult to accept that I am now alive and have to keep living all anew till I die again. And dying is always all alone even when you are surrounded by loved ones. However, maybe not now, second time around. It may feel different when it happens. I will be lucky if I go peacefully while all loved ones are with me and have come to terms with losing me.

I wrote this book in the hope that it might help others undergoing a similar journey. As the saying goes, there are many paths up the mountain. Each of us will follow our own, and encounter different hardships along the way. Each will respond in his or her own unique way. But I hope that reading my story may provide insight into some of the difficulties that might be encountered and confidence that, with help, the hardships can be overcome. The journey is most definitely worthwhile.

Perhaps the most important people in this story will never be known to me – the family of my heart donor. How to sufficiently express one's gratitude for the gift of a second chance at life? I can only hope they understand what a precious gift that was. How aware I and my family have been of this generous gift, every moment of our life since my transplant in 2014.

My gratitude to the many doctors, nurses, therapists, administrators, and others with whom I came into contact is immeasurable. Cuts to budgets, reorganisations, staff working under incredible pressure, all have their impact on staff's ability to provide the service they would like to, but the kindness and compassion they showed is without measure. There are times when things go wrong – individuals who lack compassion, misunderstandings, lack of clarity, promised services that didn't materialise – and it is sometimes necessary to be assertive in getting one's voice heard. I am incredibly grateful to my family, especially Seema, who came with me to every appointment, and spoke up when I was not able.

As a youth, it was instilled in me that how you talk to a person, how you make them feel, is more important than any gift you can give them. That always stays with them. As I grew older, I came to my own conclusions:

The struggle between individual and non-individual priorities continues. Only a short-sighted person feels it happened at particular times in history. A little reflection shows that it's there right here, right now. Sadly, most of us prefer to focus on non-essentials and run away from difficult questions and choices by using ingenious individual, known and less-known excuses. However, it's difficult to know whether human concepts like nations, patriotism or honour, right and wrong do actually mean anything.

On the other hand love as kindness, freedom (from slavery – blindly following or having to follow under duress someone else's will, usually involving work or indulgence of some kind), not hurting someone that cannot protect themselves, (e.g. most animals, babies, most children, all young children), protecting the weak, appear to be values that have a meaning by and in themselves, that transcend national borders, even most time spans.

I realise that if nothing else is achieved by the time my body becomes lifeless, I have at least tried to unwaveringly follow the above values since early in life with more awareness and intention as I got 'older' by passing of time.

Whether fortune treats you kindly or not, in the end, life is about how you handle yourself. Mine has been a journey toward acceptance – not accepting passively something that is clearly wrong – but finding peace through acceptance of those things we can't change. I learned in a visceral way the truth of Shantideva's words: *If you can solve the problem, then what is the need of worrying? If you cannot solve it, then what is the use of worrying?*' The greatest acceptance of all is the acceptance of something that will come to every one of us, however we get there – our mortality.

But enough of philosophy – I will always be grateful, but let's face it, I am just an ordinary guy who loves the sedentary life of a connoisseur, gourmet, P G Wodehouse books, and an armchair critic of good sports and entertainment programmes. Even with the blessing of good health, none of us knows how long we have left on this earth. When I reach the end of my journey, I intend to have lived my life to the full. As the saying goes, 'I want to live before I leave'. Wherever your journey takes you, I hope you do too.

Epilogue
(Seema)

'When life comes along and shakes you (which will happen), whatever is inside you will come out. It is easy to fake it until you are rattled.

Then we have to ask ourselves ... 'What is in my cup?' When life gets tough, what spills over? Joy, gratitude, peace, humility? Anger, bitterness, victim mentality and quitting tendencies?

Life provides the cup; YOU choose how to fill it. Today, let us work towards filling our cups with gratitude, forgiveness, joy, words of affirmation, resilience, positivity; and kindness, gentleness and love for others.'

Austin Tang

Diwali, a Hindu festival that brings hope and light into everyone's life, last year threw us into a deep vortex of darkness instead. Rajeev had been experiencing fever,

---

[6]Austin Tang 2021, You are holding a cup of coffee when someone comes along and bumps into you… , accessed 210823, https://goodnewsplanet.com/overcoming-obstacles-relationships/

headaches, fatigue and loss of appetite since 23rd October 2022. We thought it must be a reaction to the flu and covid vaccines taken together. The surgery recommended paracetamol. However, his temperature was not going down, and the fatigue was increasing.

On the night of 24th October, we had dinner and Rajeev said he would retire upstairs. He looked exhausted and drowsy. I made some fresh lemonade in case he was dehydrated, and kept it at his bedside. He was sitting on his bed, awake. He looked so tired. At 11 pm, he tried to pass urine and told me he could not. I was worried, called my friend. He suggested calling 111. The 111 person took details and wished to speak to Rajeev. Rajeev said he was too tired and murmured, 'I will be fine by tomorrow'. The 111 operator said she would ask a doctor to give us a call back. I asked Rajeev to lie down and said maybe a nap would help. My dear, tired husband lay his head on the pillow. Around 12 am, I sensed that the room was quiet and realised that Rajeev was not breathing. I called 999 and, by the time I started resuscitating, the ambulance had arrived. Rajeev was in a coma for the next four days and passed away peacefully on the 30th of October. He was the centre of my universe.

It has been ten months since that fateful evening. The house is so quiet now. The rest of the world carries on as usual. Time waits for no-one. The seasons come and go. Today would have been Rajeev's birthday.

Grief is a funny thing. Waves of nostalgia keep pounding the shores of one's mind. Nostalgia: *the suffering caused by an unappeased yearning to return*. How can one return? Impossible. Therefore, we cling on to the memories. I am grateful that I have so many; they keep flooding back every moment. Happy birthday Rajeev. You were special. I admire the way you handled yourself through all the adversities in life and did not break. Today, I promise to make you proud of me, to continue your legacy of helping others and making every day count.

* * *

On 30th October 2022, I lost my soulmate. A compassionate, soft-spoken, brilliant mind and a gentle man. It is hard to believe that we will not see, talk to, and hear him again. I do not know how to live without him and I am going to miss him so much. However, I know he would not want me to give up.

I am so proud to be his wife. He was not only a husband but also my true friend, a teacher and guide, a soulmate who I followed and looked up to, every step of the way all my life. We were married for thirty-six years, and he was so strong in every respect that I have never needed any other support.

There are two ways to be on this earth for humans. One is to exist; the other is to live. Existing refers to remaining alive or continuing to be. In simple terms, it is doing whatever is necessary to be alive. Living, on the other hand, means to enjoy your life and savour every moment of it. In other words: 'Passion is what you love doing and Passion pursued is Living'. By this definition, I can say that Rajeev's was a life really well lived and that, by taking everyone along with him on that journey, he made sure he was there for everyone.

I am glad that Rajeev decided to write about his journey. Publishing his book honours his memory and all the troubles he went through, and is an attempt to reach those who have opted for an organ donation and those who are in need of an organ. Having the transplant gave us eight bonus years together. Our son-in-law, Alex, had a chance to spend close time with his father-in-law. We took each day of those bonus years as it came, made the most of it, and really lived it, loved it and cherished it.

The generous gift of a life

As Rajeev's wife, I am so grateful to the donor's family for their generosity in giving this precious gift of life to my beloved husband. We owe a debt of gratitude to them, and the wonderful team of doctors and nurses at the hospital where he received his heart transplant, for giving him some much-needed time together with his family. It also gave him a few more years of delivering what he loved doing professionally. I want his donor's family to know that his heart went to the most deserving person, who received it graciously and carried on helping others until his last breath, who made the world around him a better place by making a difference to so many people's lives. Our holidays to Japan, USA, Egypt and the locations of our favourite Scandi noir are such treasured memories, and were only possible because of the transplant.

Rajeev loved me unconditionally and never hurt me with a single word. He brought out the best qualities in me. He encouraged and supported me in gaining my qualifications in fine arts and later in sociology, believing in me more than I did myself. He shared his love of music, books and movies with me and was happy to let me share my love of art with him. He was a connoisseur of food and wine and it complimented my passion for cooking. All this was only possible because of the transplant.

It made it possible for him to help many who needed his help and expertise during his eight 'bonus years'. It was as if the one act of kindness, of organ donation, had a ripple effect, touching the lives of hundreds of others. How amazing is that?

Rajeev had his transplant in 2014 and went through four rejection episodes in the first year; the psychological side effects were a shock to us. In 2016, a Facebook support group came into existence. Until then, we were not able to talk or seek support from fellow transplantees. We thought everyone went through the same difficulties as us. In 2016, when we realised that Rajeev was one of only five per cent who survived such a difficult first year, it was a surprise, but also a relief that not everyone has to go through what we did.

I want his book to reach every person who is undergoing a similar journey, and help him or her feel that they are not alone. It might not be easy with all the vicissitudes and the continuous roller coaster of emotions. However, all of that is worth it, and not in vain, for the precious bonus years for the recipient and their family.

Counting our blessings

All migrants who arrive in the UK are grateful for the life we lead and the opportunities we have as British citizens, and are always conscious of fulfilling our obligations towards our destination country. However, we also bear the tremendous burden of leaving our parents behind. Rajeev was very close to his parents and fulfilled all their emotional needs. He visited them often. However, not being there physically for them is a sad part of a migrant's life.

In addition to his family responsibilities, working for the NHS in a high-pressured job comes with its responsibilities and challenges. The demands of the job do take a toll on one's health. However, Rajeev was fortunate to have wonderful colleagues everywhere he worked and dear, close friends who were there by his side in the middle of the night when he needed them.

I do not have enough words to describe how lucky we are in the UK to have our wonderful National Health Service. The heart transplant hospital, which looked after Rajeev, with all the dedicated, hardworking and sincere doctors, nurses and all the allied health workers, had the best care possible. Being first generation migrants, and not having any family around us, it could have been a very lonely journey for us.

But the transplant team, being a specialist service, understood what we were going through, and were so kind and supportive, that we never felt alone. They always did their best to answer all our queries and offer reassurances.

It takes a lot of courage to share your story. Rajeev has shared his story bravely and honestly, just as it was, and it might just be the thing someone else might need to open their heart to hope.

Reminiscences of Rajeev from friends and family

After my dad's passing, reading his diary entries and looking back over the journey that he went on, I realise there was so much that I did not understand. We all have our own lives, our own issues that we are focussed on, progressing our own life paths. For me, during the eight years of my dad's transplant journey and the years before that when his health was at its poorest, I was graduating, getting engaged, getting married, and moving my entire life to the island of Guernsey to live with my now husband. Of course I was aware of what my parents were going through, but they took great pains in hiding the worst from us, to protect us. I also think that stressful times like this require some level of denial in order to survive, putting it to the back of the mind could be something of a defence mechanism.

Of course, the person who was directly affected was my dad. I would write, he suffered the most. But looking at him, at his smiling face, at his joy, suffering doesn't quite feel like the right word. Despite the prolonged physical and mental ordeal, he found pleasure in the simplest things. His family was of utmost importance to him, and he would take any chance he could to spend time with us. I suppose while another man may obsess over accumulating money, or assets, his brush with mortality had brought with it a wisdom about what is truly important in life; relationships, love, and time spent together making memories.

This wouldn't be complete without a mention of my mother. The phrase, behind every great man stands a great woman, comes to mind. Only with a few more adjectives added; she is loyal, enduring, loving, and steadfast. To think of the mental load she must have endured in raising two young children while dealing with everything else, as well as protecting us from the harsh realities, blows my mind. They were a team, even when divided across continents their spirit remained together. So much so, that we had taken to lovingly referring to them not as aaee (meaning mother) and baba (meaning father), but as "Aaeeba" - the entity. Reading the book, it occurred to me that my feelings towards my parents are reminiscent of my dad's feelings towards his. The guilt of not being able to do enough, being far away in another country, unable to ever repay them for everything they have given me. Perhaps it is inevitable that children feel this way, and the cycle continues on.

I look back now with many emotions; grief, sadness, and yearning for the future that will never come to pass. But surprisingly, and pleasantly, the most abundant feeling is that of gratitude; I am so thankful for everything this great man did for our family. Whether it was by conscious choice, learned as part of his chosen career, or simply in his nature, he gave us everything we needed; empathy, a listening ear, space to grow and learn and form our own identities and opinions without imposing his own vision for us on us. He made us feel that we were the most important thing in his life, worthy of love and attention. When we inevitably made mistakes, he gave us a soft place to fall, free of judgement and scorn. Every time I look at a photo or reminisce about memories with my dad, the words that come to my mind are 'Thank you'.

Ruchi Cross, Daughter

When I think of my dad, endless beautiful memories spring to mind, as well as some painful ones. I was so lucky to be able to spend a lot of quality time with him at various points of his transplant journey. Two of the most memorable and impactful times were both of my university graduation ceremonies; Swansea in the summer of 2013, and Edinburgh in 2017. Of course, I was incredibly lucky that my parents would always travel and come to support me, with no questions asked.

When I graduated in Swansea in June 2013, my dad looked quite slim and gaunt compared to his usual self. At the time, I barely even realised the amount of hardships and pain my dad must have been going through. He never let it show in front of me, and never wanted me to feel bad about it. Despite the beautiful photos we took together, packed with proud smiles and happiness, there is a deep sense of guilt I feel about times like these. Part of me wishes I would have empathised more, asked him about his struggles and his journey more. However, I'm still so happy we got to spend these moments together.

Another more recent memory which stands out to me was the surprise garden party my family threw for my thirtieth birthday! We called it a "dosa party", as my parents hired a South Indian chef to make delicious "dosas" (crispy, savoury Indian pancakes). It was a complete and utter surprise for me; the garden was packed to the brim with family friends, and even friends of mine who had sneakily been invited! My sister Ruchi made a custom cake for me, with several photos of me as a baby and teenager. It genuinely blew me away and moved me that I had a family who would do this for me!

I remember this was in August 2022, and one of the last grand, joyful memories I was able to spend with my dad. He was on top form then; not gaunt or weak at all, compared to the Swansea trip. Constantly socialising with various family friends, popping open the champagne, wishing me a happy birthday and encouraging me to mingle with everyone. It was mind-blowing to think this was a man who had undergone a serious heart transplant years prior. Even though he was on borrowed time, he was always able to be grounded in the moment and live life to the fullest. I still admire that about him so much. I miss him deeply with all of my heart, and I wish we could have spent even more amazing moments together like the dosa party. There is never enough time in life; please appreciate your loved ones and try to make each moment count.

Suhrud Banhatti, son

When the hidden sorrows of the heart spill over through copious tears

Weeping, however long it lasts, is the first step toward healing

(Article published on www.medium.com, 7th November 2022)

Two lines from the chorus of 'It's my Party':

It's my party and I'll cry if I want to
You would cry too if it happened to you

Lesley Gore

I've cried at parties, too, in hotel rooms, weddings, exam results, and unexpected gifts.

Two days ago was the last time I cried. All afternoon, I wept. Over a bottle of wine, the tears streamed during the evening, although I know the truth of the Psalmist's words: '*He heals the broken-hearted, and bandages their wounds*'. (Psalm 147:3, NIV)

When I heard he was critically ill, I resolved to hide my concerns at the bleak prognosis with optimism.

The nights were restless, and when I awoke, I hoped against hope that he would be awake. I quickly scanned my messages, noting the absence of an email from his family with relief. No news was hopeful, giving us time for a miracle as I prayed.

Four days later, I saw the subject matter, 'Sad news', and knew. He had died, but his death was not the first time I cried about him.

The first time was on my return to England after relocating. My best friend, Sue, and I were visiting him and his wife. Four friends partied, creating new memories. Gaily we decided to toast each other.

'To long life!' shouted Sue.

A chill came over us as he gently refused to join our toast. 'You three go ahead.'

He didn't think long life was on the cards for him. We tried to cover up his uncertainty about his prospects by quickly toasting our family and friends,

After a lovely visit, he and his wife took me to the airport. We were early. I'd checked in and preferred to wait with them rather than at the departure gate. Suddenly, he disappeared and did not rejoin us when I was ready to leave.

Concerned, I turned to his wife.

'He's crying', she said. 'He thinks he will never see you again.'

Her explanation for his absence shocked me. I reassured her.

He'd be okay. Of course, he'd see me again. You know men. We forced the laughter as we hugged farewell.

She did not know that as soon as she could no longer see me, I started crying. I cried during take-off and halfway across the Atlantic as I faced facts. Her husband was becoming frailer. While in his forties, his heart was failing him.

Societies prioritize family. Those of us blessed with a loving one know that life has gifted us with an invaluable resource. The time-worn saying: 'blood is thicker than water' is still true, but blood can clot with disastrous consequences while water is consistent.

In a highly mobile society, increasing numbers of people live away from their families. This trend, along with smaller families, social media, and remote working, increases loneliness. Data from CIGNA 2022 also suggests that race, gender, income, and education may play a part in the higher reports of isolation.

Therefore, finding support from people with whom we are compatible is important for our mental and physical well-being. Despite its benefits, real friendships are often overlooked and undervalued.

I met my friend at work about twenty-five years ago. He was an Indian Hindu, friendly and brilliant. His delight in his young family warmed my heart, and I volunteered as a babysitter. They, like me, had no relatives in England. Lonely people finding families is nothing new. The psalmist declared millennia ago: '*God settles the lonely in families…*' (Psalm 68:3 NIV).

Little did I know when I met him and his wife that I had found another family that would enlarge my biological one. I could not have imagined how our hearts and lives would be entwined.

Each friend loves us in different ways. These friends loved me like family. To report the death of a best friend underestimates my loss.

So I cried over the loss to myself.

Three examples of his empathy and caring indicate the extent of my loss:

• He surprised me by taking a day off his busy schedule to accompany me to a medical appointment. As a specialist, he wanted to ensure I received the best care.

• His response was no less supportive when he heard I was relocating to be closer to my biological family: 'You do have us. Move to our city so we would be close when you need us, as you age.'

• He and his precious wife came to support me before my husband's difficult heart surgery in 2018. He offered me financial help with the medical bills. I gratefully declined, touched beyond words as his illness had forced his early retirement.

I cried because of the pain of his wife and children.

His death reminded me of the indescribable pain when I lost my partner. I felt helpless at the thought of their intense suffering, knowing there is nothing one can say to ease it. To think of her enduring such grief kept the tears flowing. I realize that anytime I hear of a spouse's death, it still triggers the desolation of loss.

Losing your spouse is a developmental stage in adulthood. It is a poignant part of the life cycle as it arbitrarily brings your marriage to an end. Despite its inevitability, each survivor takes a particular path to discovery and growth. But in these early days, my friend's brave wife will be fortunate to get a good night's sleep. I cried thinking of her broken, lonely nights, which is the tax we pay for sharing our hearts and lives.

I also cried for:

- The interrupted, promising professional life

- Those books that he will not write.

- Some significant milestones of his children he will not see.

- Missing the future paintings of his artistic wife.

Next week, I'll cry again when he is laid to rest

Amidst the sadness, there will be tears in the joy of remembering the lives he touched, his favorite wines, and his love of travel, as well as for a world without him.

The words of Ecclesiastes assure us that there is a time for tears. Unlike the last time I cried, I'll be prepared.

Verbiann Hardy, friend

I first met Rajeev when we were raw, teenage 1st year medical students. We were always close friends and became especially close when we met again in UK and spent a lot of time together.

I consider myself very lucky that I had chance to have a friend like Rajeev who was an exceptional human being, intensely spiritual but at the same time deeply appreciative of all the good things and little pleasures that life had to offer.

I have not met anyone else who was so warm, so generous and kind and so positive. He could always find something to enjoy in any situation no matter how bad. He had the ability to inspire anyone around him with his enthusiasms and give them the strength to cope with the challenges of the situation.

He always made sure that he had extracted the last drop of enjoyment from books, music, art, films – in fact, everything – by studying these in great detail so that he didn't miss any of the finer points.

While writing, I can picture him in his Pink Floyd *Dark Side of the Moon* T-shirt, glass of wine in hand, making his trademark, sometimes lame jokes, and laughing loudly.

He wanted to experience the full range of emotions. I remember a day when we were watching the famous Hindi film 'Anand' for the nth time on video. There is a particularly heartrending scene at the end and Seema had gone out of the room. He paused the video and called out to Seema to come back in as the scene that would make us tearful was coming up and she should come and enjoy the 'crying scene'.

His battle with ill health was a perfect reflection of his nature and he never let his illness became the main narrative of his life. He never let restrictions on his physical activity stop him from enjoying the things he liked. If he couldn't go and watch cricket and tennis matches – no problem, he would watch it on television, mobile phone and iPad – sometimes all three simultaneously!

He must have been devastated when he first came to know that he had a serious heart condition that would require a heart transplant and limit his life. Certainly, I was in a state of shock for a long time when I came to know that he would need a heart transplant.

Perhaps he expressed his anguish to Seema, but he never showed any grief to his friends. All our meetings, including ones in hospital when he was in intensive care waiting for his transplant, continued to be full of laughter and discussion of food, music, and books. Perhaps his study of meditation and Buddhist philosophy allowed him to remain so positive when everyone close to him was struggling to accept the reality. His emotional strength was enough not only to support himself but everyone around him.

My friend lived a rich and fulfilling life, always giving more than taking and managed to pack more laughter, joy and love in his and our life than humanly possible.

We sorely miss him.

Dr Sanjay Bhate, friend

Dear Rajeev,

We knew each other quite well. In fact really well. Including your enduring your love of Jeeves and my lapsed love of PG Woodhouse.

Same goes for our Marathi icons. Your continuing love affair with Gangadhar Gadgil, Pu La Deshpande and the ultimate – Baburao Arnalkar. And here I was looking at them like an old partner – *that time was great fun, but now . . . ?*

You revelled in them. I often found them relics of a bygone era. Yet I always and wished I could enjoy simple things in life once again. Like you did. Not losing them while acquiring new tastes.

Not to say you were stuck in time. Your range was vast – from English literature to Marathi Sahitya. From Bollywood music to the Blues. From Shreya Ghoshal to Bhimsen Joshi. From Kanda Bhaji to Arancini. From Tiramisu to Anjali's Shrikhand. Your discerning taste for good food and Seema's extraordinary cooking – what a combination. Every new wine I discovered, you had been there before. You were the font of knowledge with single malts. I learnt the peaties from the mellows from you. We always planned to do a Scotland tour. Our respective wives, paid lip service. Alas, it was never to be.

You were the Guru on wines and whisky. Except the red wines. I ascribed your aversion to them to your heart problems, ultimately to claim you as another victim. Time and again, Anjali and I were firm, sometimes bordering on the robust. Yet you never took offence. Hardly a paragon of the physically fit, here I was, telling you to walk and make the most of your second life. Never was there any offence intended. More so, never taken.

Our real life views were always poles apart. You with your rose-tinted vision, and me with my 'in broad daylight' sight. Our views often were chalk and cheese, our friendship always thick as thieves.

We opened our hearts to Seema and you, we looked upon you as our family away from family. So did you. Such a lovely husband you have been to Seema all these years. Everytime we met, I would get a dose of: 'how caring he is'. It never stopped me wanting to meet you.

The way Ruchi and Suhrud, as well as Alex and Pradmuyma fawned over you, not once but always. And the joy on Ruchi's face when you could attend her wedding will make every father want to be in your shoes. You have been such a good father to your children, instilling the right and the wrong, yet allowing them to fly with their own wings. You have been an excellent doctor, a child psychiatrist who cured and cared, your service much appreciated here in the UK and abroad.

No one will be lost without you more than your wife Seema. She will struggle, no doubt, the two of you so close, despite the years. Her devotion and care of you, perhaps added a few years to your sadly shortened life. The children will miss you, as always they do. Unimaginable as it may seem, life will take its course, washing all of us in the sands of time.

But here and now, Anjali and I will always miss you. I have never been a writer. I hope you can see our sorrow at your passing come through. We will always miss you. As a forever friend, as a lovely person, as a lovely doctor, as a lovely father, as a lovely husband and as a lovely human being.

Suhrud and Akshay, our children and their partners Rose and Alice share in our sorrow at your untimely death. We all wish you were still here. Nevertheless, all we can do, is to pray that Seema and your family pull through. They can always count our support if they ever need it.

Over the years, you were veering towards Buddhist philosophy, on this sad occasion let me say in the Hindu tradition:

Second Time Around

Ishwar tujhya atmyas Shanti Devo,

May God bring peace to your soul

Aanek Namaskar

Harshawardhan and Anjali Bilolikar

Thinking back on the moments I have shared with Rajeev, it's impossible not to feel a sense of warmth and cordiality for fellow humans. For me, Rajeev was a shining example of wisdom, kindness, and selflessness.

The Banhattis are our closest family friends. We have spent several evenings and weekends together in each other's company, dining, watching TV and cricket. Rajeev often invited me to watch cricket matches. I used to love his company mainly because he always had some wise words to share.

In a world often filled with self-centredness, Rajeev stood out as a beacon of empathy. He possessed a beautiful quality that made him think about others, even amid his challenges and difficulties. Rajeev showed genuine care and concern for those around him and had the magical ability to make everyone feel special. Whether it was some average dish we had cooked, a small gift we had bought for him, or a trivial achievement on our part, he always had generous and genuine words of appreciation. His ability to connect with people on a deeply personal level, to listen intently without judgement, and to offer words of support and guidance was remarkable. He knew exactly when someone needed a listening ear. Kindness was Rajeev's defining trait. His heart was full of warmth and compassion, and this radiated profusely in his company.

He made an immeasurable impact on the lives of many children and their families through his unwavering dedication to his profession of child psychiatry. He continued his work despite his illness with the same enthusiasm. There were serious concerns about acute deterioration of his health during his illness. Despite his health circumstances, he dared to spend months in Isle of Man and Guernsey doing the work he loved. He used to enjoy his public speaking adventures on various psychiatry and general topics. He would take advantage of every speaking opportunity when visiting India or when invited to speak to non-medical groups in the UK. His thirst for knowledge seemed insatiable, constantly seeking to understand the recent developments and treatments in his field of psychiatry, which I am sure has benefitted countless people. I was fascinated to listen to his insight on psychology and his work on how the human brain starts getting affected very early in the womb before birth.

His passions spanned the spectrum from English literature to music, cricket to wines. Both English literature and Hindu mythology held a special place in his heart. He seemed to devour fiction and non-fiction, novels and poetry, and contemporary literature with equal enthusiasm. At our parties among friends, he would often share his insights into his reading, sparking engaging discussions, debates and sometimes arguments in and with the best spirits. Thanks to Rajeev, I am now an avid reader of philosophy, particularly ancient Hindu philosophy. His interest in literature was a testament to his intellectual curiosity. His ability to find wisdom and solace in written words was truly remarkable.

To say that Rajeev adored cricket would be an understatement. He followed every Indian match with unwavering dedication, analysing the strategies of captains and celebrating good innings of all players, both Indian and opposing teams, with the same passion. But one thing he couldn't bear was a loss for the Indian team. He would call me to his house to watch all crucial Indian matches, particularly against Pakistan as if I were his moral support if things went badly for the Indian team. He would always have a story to tell of another brilliant innings he had watched earlier that week. Listening to his narration of the innings was as good as being present on the field and witnessing the event.

His palate was more than refined, and his ability to savour nuances of fine wine was awe-inspiring. Offer him a wine, and he would try to scrutinise the origin and, on most occasions, get it right. He would talk about how food flavour and wine aroma danced on the palate, creating a divinely choreographed experience at the dining table. He believed wine was more than a drink; it was a cultural and social experience for him. He introduced me to the world of wine. I learnt from these social evenings that life, like an elegant wine, is beautiful and could be savoured and enjoyed sip by sip. He sauvignon-ed me.

I had a friend who embraced life's rich tapestry and understood the multiplicity of tastes reflecting the diversity of perspectives and human experiences. Seeing a wide range of passions woven into Rajeev's life's fabric was genuinely terrific. He seemed to see the world through a unique lens, as if he was seeing the world from a balcony above the clouds. I sometimes wondered whether his near-death experiences meant he wore a different lens. Some people have the knack of hawk-eye view, and Rajeev seemed to be graced with that divine gift.

His absence leaves a void that can never be truly filled. He showed us that a well-lived life is enriched by a library of wisdom, a cellar of experiences, a stadium of hopes and a symphony of varied interests. I was fortunate to have Rajeev as my friend for many years. I have missed him, and the loss is irreparable. But the thoughts about Rajeev are always positive and will remain a sense of warmth in my heart forever.

Dr Prashant Kakodkar, Friend